HOPE
REFRESHED

Modern Parables Collection Book 1

~ Bible Parables Retold ~

Robert Goluba

Bible quotations are from the New International Version (NIV). Copyright © 1973, 1978, 1984 by International Bible Society

ISBN: 1514328038
ISBN 13: 9781514328033

Hope Refreshed is part thought provoking, part educational, and part entertainment. It is a collection of powerful Bible parables that have been refreshed and retold to show how messages of hope, grace, love, forgiveness, and redemption in scripture still apply over two thousand years later.

Hope Refreshed is written for all readers, regardless of faith or religious background. Some will pick up on the parables early in the story and recognize that their excerpts still deliver highly relevant, good news today. Others will simply enjoy a short story with messages of hope, love, forgiveness, redemption, and grace woven throughout the pages. All readers will have a better understanding of how these classic stories and parables, with their timeless messages, still apply today. Some may even gain more hope at a time when it might seem a little distant. That's hope refreshed!

CONTENTS

INTRODUCTION

O ver the past four decades, I have witnessed and experienced a lot of different things. One conclusion that I have settled on from all this life experience is that we are all different. Shocking, I know! We each have different fears, dreams, likes, and dislikes; we each learn differently and come to faith differently. This epiphany struck me one morning while sitting in the back of the classroom and assisting the fifth- and sixth-grade preteen ministry at Sun Valley Community Church in Gilbert, Arizona, several years ago.

Patrick Hodgkins was the instructor. I was amazed at how engaged the kids were when he would break down complicated but important Bible stories and parables with stories of his own that the preteens could understand easily. Guess what? As a forty-year-old, I was also learning from Bible stories that I had heard many times but still did not grasp completely until I heard them retold to a room of fifth and sixth graders. Not only were we all entertained (Patrick is an amazing storyteller), but we were also educated and enlightened; I believe the former led to the latter. That's when it hit me:

Maybe more people would understand the important messages within the Bible if they learned them in a way they could understand or grasp just a little better.

At that moment, I decided to retell Bible parables and stories in a way that was entertaining and educational. That way, all readers could get the powerful messages of hope, grace, love, forgiveness, and redemption that might create a thirst to read the original scripture in the Bible.

I chose to write short stories in *Hope Refreshed,* so virtually anyone can read an entire story and get a quick dose of hope in twenty to thirty minutes.

Note: In no way does Hope Refreshed intend to add to, subtract from, or change scripture. Scripture is perfect and does not need to be changed. My objective is to use parallel stories to spark interest in reading original scripture for the first, fortieth, or four-hundredth time.

For years after that fateful day in the back of the classroom, I thought about how I would retell the stories. One morning, I woke up a little after 5:00 a.m. with an entire story in my head. Luckily it was a weekend, so I sat at my computer for eight hours until seven thousand words were on my screen. I thank the Holy Spirit for those words because they were far too creative to be mine.

Once I completed the first draft of my first story, I knew I had to write more stories and publish them for others to enjoy. That was the genesis of *Hope Refreshed*. I hope you enjoy reading it as much as I enjoyed writing it!

JUDGMENT DAY

His hands were shaking so badly that John could hardly take a sip of water. He loosened his tie, hoping it would relieve the pressure building in his neck and chest. It was his turn at the podium, and he knew he had to bring his A-game.

John was campaigning to be chairman of a state political party—something he had dreamed of since graduating from college with a degree in political science. He had been involved with the party and running campaigns for the past eleven years, so he knew he was qualified. But his challenger, Brian, liked to intimidate his competitors.

Brian was six foot three and over 230 pounds, so he was physically imposing. Brian was also skilled at verbal intimidation, so John was not surprised when verbal punches were thrown at him. Brian had held several elected offices in the past and was well-known for smearing the opposition as a campaign tactic.

"I want to thank each and every one of you for allowing me to pursue my dream of becoming your party chairman," John started after pushing aside his fear. "You just heard from the opposing candidate. He gave you a laundry list of reasons why you should not vote for me—and very few reasons why you should vote for him. I am going to approach this from a different angle. I am going to tell you why I am the best candidate to run this party without ever mentioning another name."

John felt a boost in confidence as he noticed some murmurs and nods from the audience. He cleared his throat, pushed up his glasses, and stood up tall to accentuate all six feet of his frame before continuing. "Let me start by saying that, first and foremost; I want to bring trust, transparency, and ethics back to this party..."

John went on for over fifteen minutes outlining his plans for turning the party around. His slight midwestern accent was most evident when he got excited about a topic. The audience was in awe. John was easy to like. He was articulate, confident, and convincing; his listeners genuinely believed he could make their party better. More important, they felt he could lead them to a decisive yet clean victory in the upcoming state elections.

After leaving the podium, John went backstage and waited for the results.

"Hunter, any idea on when the final tally will be in?" John asked his twenty-year-old hipster assistant.

"Nope," Hunter replied without looking up from his cell phone.

"It has to be pretty soon. I finished speaking over an hour ago. You would think that—"

Hunter interrupted. "They just texted me. The votes are in, and we should all head back out to the stage."

Again, John was nervous but confident. His approach had paid off. By a landslide—68 percent of the votes—his party had elected him to be their state chairman for the next four years. John's fiancée, Charlotte, ran up to him and wrapped her arms around his neck. She stood on the tips of her pumps so she could give him a congratulatory kiss. "I'm so proud of you!" she said.

John and Charlotte had met nine months earlier at a church fundraiser. He was immediately struck by her beauty, inside and out. Charlotte had long black hair, bronze skin, and the most amazing smile John had ever seen. Plus, the two shared many hobbies and similar values. John's respect for her was deep, especially because at only twenty-nine years old, Charlotte had already experienced a broken marriage, yet she was as confident and strong as anyone he had ever met.

Charlotte married her college sweetheart the year after they graduated. Two years into the marriage, she found out about his multiple extramarital affairs. Counseling did not help, so Charlotte found herself divorced by her mid-twenties. John admired that she was neither angry at, nor bitter toward, any man, including her ex. Instead, she found forgiveness in the aftermath of the divorce. Charlotte was young and knew that, eventually, the right guy would come along and that they would get married and start a family.

John wished he had that kind of confidence. His story regarding relationships was very different; only a few girlfriends had gotten past the third or fourth date. It had not mattered much because John was so driven to prove himself as the next young political guru that his work consumed his life. Before John knew it, he was turning thirty and still as unattached as ever...until Charlotte came into his life.

John was nervous about proposing to Charlotte after only seven months of dating, but he didn't want to put off what he believed to be inevitable. Everything was different with Charlotte. John had no question that he wanted to spend the rest of his life with her. Only two months before the party election, she accepted his proposal.

Late one night in his office at the party headquarters, John questioned aloud what he'd gotten himself into—not with Charlotte; he loved her, of course. The chairman position was making him feel more overwhelmed than ever before. John had gone to work immediately in his new post because, as a man of his word, he was determined to deliver on all his campaign promises. But even he was surprised at the amount of backstabbing and infighting that took place within his party. John knew this was what he'd signed up for, so he did his best to guide his party through all the storms. What John didn't expect was that he would be spending less time with Charlotte.

John pulled out his phone and texted her: *Late again. So sorry about all of this. Love you.*

Charlotte responded: *I understand. Some things are worth waiting for.*

John: *What did I do to deserve you?*

Charlotte: *You are a lucky man. God must really like you.*

John laughed out loud and replied: *LOL. He must. Going now so I can hurry over after I'm done here.*

At that moment, John realized that all of the political office drama was worth bearing because he could do something special in his job—make a positive and lasting change in the state he loved. Charlotte supported him, and that was all the support he needed.

John quickly wrapped up the notes for his next speech and fired off his last e-mail of the evening. Primary season was getting into full swing. He needed to guide his party through a contentious primary without each candidate for governor bludgeoning the other too badly before the general election.

He locked the office door behind him and noticed he was walking faster than normal to his car. John was going to Charlotte's apartment, and he could not wait to see her.

The Sinner

John arrived at his office early every morning. He liked to check the latest polls and catch up on the news. He did not like surprises, and he preferred to be left alone until 8:00 a.m., so he looked up, annoyed when Hunter burst into his office at 7:50 a.m.

Hunter asked, "Did you hear the news?"

"What news?" John replied tersely.

"Brian announced he's going to run for governor. He's jumping into the primary!" Hunter wore a smug look on his face. It was rare that he had any news that John hadn't heard already, so Hunter seemed proud of this little nugget.

"How did you find this out?" John asked, perplexed.

"He texted me on my way into the office. He said that he's going to be the next governor of this state and that my boss had better find some funds for his campaign. I checked with my friend down at the television news desk, and apparently Brian has a press conference scheduled for ten o'clock on the courthouse stairs to announce his candidacy."

John felt like he'd been punched in the stomach. He had been working so hard to run a well-orchestrated primary, and the candidates John had endorsed were honorable people. Most party members were buying into John's program of ethics, honesty, and transparency as the new pillars of the party. John suspected all of that might change with Brian entering the race, so he was both nervous and angry.

"John, I've heard this is one cutthroat dude," Hunter chimed in. "I heard he sued a widow when she tried to back out of her pledge when he was running for mayor. The word is that a couple made a large donation to Brian, but the husband died in an accident shortly after they sent the check. The wife wanted the money back to help cover funeral expenses. Brian sued her to keep the money, and he won. I don't know how much lower someone can get than suing a poor old widow!"

"Hunter, I'm not sure if that's even true. Don't repeat that to anyone else."

"OK, boss. I'm going to open the file on Brian and get some work done."

"Thank you, Hunter. Please shut the door behind you."

John leaned back in his chair to gaze at the ceiling. He stared for a few minutes before looking back at the e-mails on his computer screen, realizing he could not concentrate enough to be productive.

He left the office and drove downtown, parking his car near the courthouse. He saw news crews setting up cameras and microphones in anticipation of Brian's press conference. John could not believe this was happening. He needed some perspective, so he called

Charlotte at Bright Smiles Family Dentistry where she worked as a dental hygienist. She answered her cell phone immediately.

"Hey, John, what's up? Is everything OK?"

"Sure, why would you ask that?"

"Because you usually don't call me this early unless something is wrong or bothering you," Charlotte said in her usual, soothing manner.

"You know me so well." John was already starting to feel a little better, just from hearing her voice. "Do you remember Brian—the guy I ran against for party chairman? The one who said all those negative things about me?"

"Yes, I remember him. How could I not?"

"Well, he's decided to jump into the governor's race. What was supposed to be a productive and civil primary is going to be in the gutter within minutes of Brian announcing his candidacy. This guy is a slimeball and a snake. Now he wants me to help him fund his negative campaign against other candidates who are far more qualified. I'm so angry right now I don't know what to do!" John was starting to lose his breath after talking so fast.

"First of all, relax. You'll get through this," Charlotte said calmly.

"OK, but I still don't know what I am going to do."

"Keep doing what you have been doing," Charlotte said without pause.

"What do you mean by that?"

"You have a plan that's been working, and everyone else seems to be on board. So why let one guy who has not bought into the plan derail your progress? He'll look silly when he's the only one with a negative campaign, so don't waver. Stick to the plan!"

John knew she was right. He had a ton of support from the candidates, his staff, and—most importantly—many big donors. He didn't have a choice about Brian entering the race, but he could continue to implement his plan.

Let Brian expose himself for the jerk that he is, he thought.

John was confident his party voters would see through Brian.

"You're absolutely right, honey," John said, already feeling less angst.

"Dr. Pence just went in with a patient. I gotta go!"

"Sounds about as much fun as a root canal," quipped John with the joke he never got tired of telling.

"Two implants on both sides of her mouth. It's going to take a couple of hours, so I'll see you later tonight. Bye."

"OK. Bye."

Reinvigorated, John called each of the candidates to tell them Brian was entering the race. They had varying initial reactions as John assured them that he was committed to running a productive primary in which the party's candidate would emerge strong against the opposing party's challenger. One candidate expressed a desire to go on the offensive against Brian, but ultimately he committed to staying the course with John. John was dedicated to the plan, and these fine candidates trusted him.

After talking with Charlotte, John was even more emboldened to work with some key donors to raise additional money for all candidates, including Brian.

A month later, the party held its first debate. Everything went as John had envisioned it. Brian went on the attack against the other three candidates, who redirected the questions back to their talking points and maintained a positive tone. Nevertheless, it was clear that all of these candidates felt frustrated by the personal attacks; they wanted to respond with dirt of their own on Brian. Instead, they honorably refused to allow Brian to drag them down into the mud pit with him.

John was sure the voters would see through Brian's ways and was waiting on the first polls the morning after the debate. He was so certain Brian would be trailing in the polls that he yelled, "No way!" when he saw the results. Brian had jumped to second place behind the front-runner, Maya Chopra, and was a full ten points ahead of Andrew Newman, who was now third. John could not believe it. Not only were his assumptions on the debate results wrong, but now he also second-guessed his whole strategy for a clean campaign. He knew others felt the same way and would be calling him soon to voice their dissatisfaction. John remembered his conversation with Charlotte a month earlier, and he intended to stay the course.

John had a long day—he took call after call from candidates, reporters, and donors who questioned his strategy to run a clean campaign. John gave his best effort to sell his approach, and it worked. Once again, he convinced everyone that the results of the first debate were just temporary and that Brian would soon fall back in the polls.

The Judgment

For the next couple of weeks, John spent his days working on the primary campaigns and nights helping Charlotte plan for their wedding. Though John often had a hard time breaking away from work, he felt comfortable enough to sneak in a couple of meetings with the caterer and the wedding photographer one afternoon. He wanted to support Charlotte during the wedding planning because she always supported him.

John was just leaving the country club that would be hosting the wedding reception when he received an unexpected call from Andrew's campaign manager, Carl.

"John, are you in the office right now?"

"No, but I am on my way. What's up?"

"I found out some information on Brian that will shut him up and get him out of the race permanently."

Carl sounded giddy before blurting out, "Brian is having an affair with one of his interns. We have pictures, text messages, and e-mails, and the best part is that Brian's wife doesn't even know. That arrogant jerk is going to wish he never set foot in this race!"

Stunned, John paused. "How do you know this is legit? Are you positive this information is accurate?"

Carl responded quickly, "Revenge! The boyfriend of the intern found everything on her phone and forwarded it to one of our staffers. He said he assumed we would know what to do with it. It's all right there, John. The e-mails, texts—everything!"

"What do you intend to do with it, Carl?"

"I've already reached out to Maya's campaign manager and just spoke with Andrew. We all plan to come down to your office tomorrow morning at ten so we can launch a coordinated counterattack against Brian and share this with the media."

John had a million things swirling in his head and could only muster, "OK, see you tomorrow."

John's head was spinning after hearing this news. He was committed to running a clean campaign, but he was also tired of cheaters like Brian; he thought of Charlotte and how her first marriage had ended due to her ex-husband's infidelities. John began to wonder if leaking this information would send a clear message to Brian and other dishonest men like him. He reasoned to himself; *It's done all the time in politics. Nobody would ever have to know I was involved.*

Even as he was convincing himself that the smear was the right way to go with this, John felt uneasy about the tactics. He justified it to himself, thinking, *Brian deserves to be put in his place.*

John texted Charlotte: *Really need to talk to you tonight about something at work. What should I bring over for dinner?*

John was sure Charlotte would agree with him. After all, Brian was a cheating snake. John figured she might feel some justice in seeing a cheater pay a price for the hurt he inflicted on others. John decided it was worth leaking the scandal if it could deliver an impactful message that cheating is wrong, even in politics.

John showed up at Charlotte's apartment with their favorite Chinese takeout.

"So what's bothering you?" Charlotte asked as she filled plates with shrimp lo mein and Szechuan green beans.

They sat at the dining table, chopsticks in hand. Between bites, John explained the whole situation to Charlotte.

"We're having a meeting tomorrow morning. Our plan is to leak the information to the media." He looked closely at Charlotte, expecting to see some sign of agreement.

Instead, she asked, "Why would you do that?"

"I have to be honest, Charlotte. I kind of thought you'd be happy to hear this. After all, your ex cheated on you. Somebody needs to send a message to these cheaters."

"I don't want revenge on my ex or anyone else for that matter. I'm also sure you're not doing his wife any favors by dragging her into the spotlight with such embarrassing and hurtful news. As a matter of a fact, I've forgiven my ex for cheating on me. You know that," Charlotte said quietly looking into John's eyes.

"I do know, but I don't understand it. How can you do that, Charlotte? I could never forgive someone who did that to me."

"It wasn't easy, but I did it for me, not him. Remember that Jesus wants us to offer grace to people who make mistakes. He showed mercy even for those who crucified him."

John, clearly annoyed, replied, "I know, I know. I've been going to church for thirty years, and I know all about the grace of Jesus." He stood up and walked to the window. Like his feelings regarding the campaign, he wasn't happy about the direction this conversation was taking.

Charlotte broke the momentary silence. "Do you really know about grace? I mean, do you really know about forgiving someone who has hurt you—even someone you feel doesn't deserve to be forgiven? Forgiving someone who has hurt you to the core is one of the hardest things to do."

John, unresponsive, continued to look out the window.

"You never did answer my original question, John. Why are you doing this?"

John was instantly hit with a range of emotions. He was sad because Brian was ruining the clean campaign he'd spent years developing and still angry about the hurtful accusations Brian made about him while running for party chairman.

Finally, John responded as he spun around from the window. "Brian deserves it. He hurts everyone he comes into contact with, and now he's crossed the line. He's hurt Maya and Andrew, and he lied about me during the campaign for party chairman. I haven't been able to shake that, and I will not forgive him for it."

Charlotte stood up and walked over to John. She put both hands on his shoulders and, almost whispering in his ear, said, "To forgive is not to condone hurtful behavior. It simply means the debt is paid. They don't owe you anything anymore, so you can let go of the resentment and move forward with your life."

"Brian has bigger issues to confront than this campaign. You should forgive him, so you no longer feel he owes you. It's not your place to judge him. You won't be able to move forward in a positive direction until you truly forgive him."

"Honey, I hear what you're saying—but I'm still not sure what I'm going to do. Sorry, but I'm going home early tonight, so I can think about it some more." As John was clearing off the table, he said, "It's going to get ugly in my office tomorrow."

Once again, John knew Charlotte was right. Still, he was unsure of what he would do because he felt certain everyone in the meeting tomorrow would pressure him to take swift action against Brian. No matter how good of a sales pitch he could give, John couldn't fathom how everyone in that room would forgive Brian.

Charlotte was helping John clear off the table when he grabbed her and spun her around. He snapped out of his funk and flashed a big smile.

As he looked Charlotte in her brown eyes, he said, "Thanks again for being so patient with me while I complained about all this stuff at work. You always give me such great advice. What did I do to deserve you?" John kissed her.

He was heading for the door when Charlotte said, "Because God really does love you." John smiled again when he heard that. Then Charlotte said, "And he loves Brian too."

John paused before closing the door behind him.

The alarm went off at 5:25 a.m., as it did every morning, but John wasn't sure he'd actually slept at all that night. He was running through all the possible scenarios in his head, and he was still not sure what to do.

He got ready for work, and having a few spare minutes before he needed to leave, John sat down on his couch to think about the coming day. His cat, Buddy, jumped on his lap.

John started to pet the tan fur on Buddy's head and said, "I'm sorry I haven't been home very much, Buddy. I promise I'll make it up to you after the general election is over." Buddy purred in approval.

John knew the chaos would start in a few hours, so he enjoyed the peace and calm while he lay back against the pillows on his couch. Buddy quickly curled up on his chest. John's mind went to the conversation he had the night before with Charlotte about forgiveness.

God loves everyone, even the "unlovable" Brian.

John felt desperate now, so he closed his eyes and prayed for answers.

John heard the door slam across the hallway, and it startled both him and Buddy. He knew his neighbor did not leave for work until well after John did each day. John quickly realized he must have fallen asleep on the couch. He put Buddy on the couch as he jumped up and grabbed his briefcase, wallet, keys, and phone.

John arrived at the office a little after 8:00 a.m. He didn't have time for his normal morning routine, but he didn't care. All he could focus on was the ten o'clock meeting. He dealt with a quick briefing with Hunter, a conference call, and some e-mails, and then the first candidate walked into the conference room. John met him there, shook his hand, and greeted him.

"Mr. Newman. Glad to see you today."

Andrew Newman snapped back, "I wish I could say the same. I'm not any happier to be here than you are, so let's get this show on the road. Is the Chopra team here yet?"

"Not yet," said Hunter as he entered the room.

"Well, I guess when you're the front-runner, you get to set your own schedule," Andrew said with a half smile.

The room was quiet for a few minutes until Maya Chopra and her campaign manager, Amanda, arrived. Everyone stood up to greet them. They all sat down at the table, and Amanda got straight to the point.

"We've all heard the news. What are we going to do?"

"Yes, what are *we* going to do here?" The question came from the doorway.

It was Brian, and he was staring at all his accusers. Everyone looked at Brian and then at one another, not knowing how to respond.

Brian broke the stony silence with his smugness as he said, "Did you all forget this is the party headquarters of the same party I'm in? Did you think you could just hold an ambush meeting here without my knowing? No wonder I'm passing everyone in the polls. You guys aren't very smart."

Andrew's campaign manager, Carl, retorted, "Since you're so brilliant, I think you know what needs to be done here."

Brian took a step back and mockingly grabbed his chest as if he had just been shot in the heart.

He said sarcastically, "No, I don't know what needs to be done, so that's why I'm asking. What you are going to do to me?"

For the first time, John actually felt sorry for Brian. He realized Brian must be hurting to act in such a way.

What could make someone act that way? Brian pondered.

Maya interrupted his thought.

"Well, John, it's up to you now. Let us all know what we're going to do."

John felt a sense of clarity. He'd felt it since he woke up on the couch after praying earlier in the day. His conversation with Charlotte and all his thoughts of the past twenty-four hours on the best way to address the situation resulted in this epic response:

"We do nothing."

John leaned forward in his chair and closely watched the faces of everyone at the table to gauge their reactions. He even smiled a bit when he realized that confusion generated a very distinct facial expression. Everybody was baffled, including Brian.

Hunter responded first.

"Are you sure? I got everything together for my friend at TV News, and he'll never divulge his source. Is that what you're worried about?"

"No, I'm not worried about covering our tracks," John replied. "I think we should forgive Brian and move on as if this never happened."

Suddenly, everyone was shouting at the same time.

"Are you crazy?"

"Haven't you heard what he has said about *us*?"

"Why would we forgive him after all this?"

John felt an inner strength as he stood up to stop everyone.

"Frankly," he said, "a part of me would like to see Brian swallow a fat dose of his own bitter medicine. However, I said from the very beginning that I want to run an honorable campaign. The honorable thing to do is forgive Brian and move on."

John sat back down and noticed he had spilled some water from his glass when he had abruptly stood up. He gave the spilled water his full attention as he was swirling his finger in the small puddle next to his glass. Then John noticed the shimmering shadow his glass of water cast on the table from the sun peering through the east-facing windows. John smiled as he realized he had been in hundreds of meetings in this room. But for the first time, he noticed how interesting the wall looked as sunlight hit the table and reflected onto the pictures on the wall.

Andrew noticed John was scribbling imaginary words on the table with his finger. This frustrated Andrew even more, so he threw his hands into the air.

"Forgive him?" Andrew said. "He has lied, cheated, and said horrible things about all of us. Grow a spine, John. If you don't have the guts to make the call, we will."

John stopped scribbling on the table.

He snapped back up, "Really? Then I invite any one of you in this room who has never lied, cheated, twisted the truth, or stepped on someone else for your own political gain to send the packet of pictures to the media!" John sat back down, glaring.

Andrew turned to his campaign manager, Carl.

"Obviously, John is not going to do anything about this. I have things to do, so let's get to my next appointment." The two stood up and left without another word.

Maya Chopra's campaign manager, Amanda, was the next to address John.

"I think you're making a big mistake on this one. Running a clean campaign is one thing, but feeding the fox so it doesn't leave the hen house is another. I hope we don't all live to regret this."

John replied, "Mrs. Chopra is the front-runner and will make an excellent governor. You don't want to win this way. Let's do it the right way."

Maya and Amanda offered politely forced smiles before they got up and left.

Hunter, Brian, and John were the only three left in the room.

Hunter looked at John and said, "What do you want me to do with the packet, boss? I have all of the incriminating evidence right here."

"Give it to Brian," John said without hesitation.

Hunter reluctantly turned over the packet to Brian and left the room.

Brian was still standing near the doorway where he made his dramatic entrance only a few minutes earlier.

Still looking puzzled, he asked John, "Why are you doing this? What do you expect to gain?"

"Ab-so-lute-ly nothing," John said slowly while never losing eye contact with Brian. "I think you should leave now. Go home, and look yourself in the mirror. You're at a crossroads now, so be completely honest with yourself."

Brian stood in the doorway still stunned. He opened his mouth to say something but stopped. Speechless, he turned around and left.

John was physically and mentally exhausted from the confrontation. He wanted to see Charlotte. He met her for lunch and told her what had unfolded. John was back to his original clean-campaign plan, and Charlotte was proud of his decision.

A week after the confrontation in the conference room, Brian showed up in John's office doorway unannounced late one afternoon. He was unshaven and looked like he had slept in his clothes. John was a little worried that he might have come to the office to exact revenge for feeling ridiculed. Brian stood silently and glared at John. Brian's large frame blocked any escape through the doorway. John contemplated whether he should duck for cover.

Finally, Brian said, "I'm done. I'm ruined."

John, still nervous about Brian's intentions, said, "I'm sorry things turned out this way, but—"

Brian interrupted, "I want to thank you for what you did."

Now John was confused. "You do?"

"I told my wife. I told her everything. We've been married twenty-three years, and this was not the first time I cheated. She was not as forgiving as you are, so she kicked me out. I've been sleeping in my car the last two nights," Brian said with a slight chuckle. "I also looked in the mirror, like you said. I avoided doing that for years because I knew I wouldn't like what I saw."

Brian plopped down in one of John's chairs at his desk and continued.

"My father was really, really tough on me growing up and I also felt very weak and ashamed. I vowed never to be weak again and that I would do anything I could—and I mean anything—so I would be strong.

"I've always known it was there, but I've been running from it for so long that I've never had to face it, and frankly I didn't mind hurting others. Most of them were jerks like me, and I figured they probably deserved it. However, this time, I hurt the one person who truly loved me for who I really am.

"I have to fix this and make it right with my wife, no matter what it takes, so I'm dropping out of the race and getting out of politics." Brian started to cry. "I'm sorry about all the stuff I said about you. I still can't believe what you did after everything I said about you. Nobody has ever forgiven me like that before, and it really hit home. I need to say 'I'm sorry' to a lot more people and forgive some people, including myself."

John said, "Brian, I hope you find what you're looking for. Life is all about relationships with people, so be sure to treat people well."

"I know. Thank you for not throwing the first stone. Now I can stop living a lie and be the kind of guy I always wanted to be—the guy I know I can be. I'm at peace with this decision." Brian stood up, turned around, and began to walk out of John's office.

"Brian—before you go, take this." John handed Brian a card for his pastor. "If you really want to work on your marriage or even just yourself first, give him a call. He has really helped me."

Brian looked at the card. He put it in his back pocket and proceeded to leave the building.

Several weeks later, before the next debate, John ran into the Chopra team backstage. Maya said she thought more about the decision John made to forgive Brian and understood that it was the right thing to do.

"It was tough, but I've forgiven him, too," she said. "The ironic thing is that *I* feel better about the whole situation now. Have you heard from Brian? What's he doing now?"

"I haven't heard from him, but I do know Brian and his wife are meeting with a pastor to try and work things out."

"You're due on stage in a few minutes. Future governor Chopra can't be late for a debate, so get going," John said as he gently pushed Maya toward the stage.

John went back out to the auditorium and found Charlotte saving a seat for him. He sat down and began smiling while staring at the empty stage.

Charlotte noticed and asked, "What's so funny?"

John looked at her and replied, "Nothing. Just happy."

Overview

This is the modern rendition of the famous story about the religious leaders trying to trap Jesus in the stoning of an adulterous woman, from John 8:2–11. Here, John takes the role of Jesus; Brian is the woman who was caught committing adultery, and the other politicians are the religious leaders who want to stone her. In both stories, the parable demonstrates how many people are often quick to judge others but do not like to look at their own sins. It also shows the power of extending grace to others who have committed sins but are willing to change and repent.

Moral of the Story: Do not judge others who sin differently than you. Forgive others, and repent your own sins.

THE GOOD SPORT

I t started out as a mild rumble...and then the ground shook as the crowd around him went crazy! Everyone in the stadium jumped, hugged, and high-fived after an interception in the end zone was returned 102 yards for a touchdown. It was always like this during the annual intrastate college football game—the traditional rivalry between the two largest universities in the state always drew a lot of fans and excitement. But because both teams were riding on winning records this year, the excitement level was exceptionally high.

Kyle turned to his friends and yelled, "Man! That was awesome. Gotta love football!"

His friend, Matt, loudly agreed. "I know! I am so glad I could make this game. Missing the last few years sucked."

Kyle and Matt were roommates at State University. Matt relocated back to the area this past summer, and he hadn't attended an in-state game for a while.

"I don't know why you wouldn't just fly back for the games," their other college buddy, Caleb, said. "I totally would if I ever had to move away. I wouldn't miss this game for anything." Caleb had continued to keep the tradition of attending the state rivalry game for all fourteen years after graduation.

"Whatever, Caleb," Matt yelled. "You say that because you played on this field, but if your job makes you relocate a thousand miles from here, it's not that easy to always get back for a game."

"You're right—I owned that end zone right down there!" said Caleb, his chest out and a big smile on his face as he stared down at the north end of the field.

"That was just one fumble recovery you ran back, so don't get too carried away," spouted Matt with a grin.

"Hey! Kickoff team is one of the most important parts of the game," Caleb yelled back. "If we don't stay in our lanes, then—"

Kyle interrupted, shouting above both of them. "Speaking of kickoff—we're about to kick off now!"

The three turned their attention back to the field while Kyle cheered. "Come on, guys. Let's pin the Eagles back, deep!"

Kyle, Matt, and Caleb had all gone to State University and were die-hard Bulldog fans. Their disdain for the downstate Eagles—and even their fans—was rampant, and the feeling was mutual. It was not uncommon for a scuffle to break out in the stands, parking lot, or bars following most games between the two teams. Back in college, the guys cheered on the fights. Now, in their thirties, they preferred to avoid the conflicts.

"Want another one?" Caleb asked his friends as he headed to get another beer. "The concession stand shuts down after the third quarter."

"Sure, if you're buying!" exclaimed Matt.

"Um, OK. I guess one more won't kill me," said Kyle.

"I doubt it, considering it would only be our second round of beers. I'm pretty sure it would make us the soberest group in this crowd. Look, don't let anything exciting happen while I'm gone," Caleb said, already running down the stadium steps.

About twenty minutes later, Caleb returned, exasperated.

"What took you so long?" Matt asked, both hands in the air.

"It's crazy down there, and a fight broke out in the beer line. It took five minutes to restore order. Then I was behind, like, thirty people. Did I miss anything?" he asked, taking his seat.

"Only three punts, and it looks like a fourth one here pretty soon," Kyle stated coolly, nodding toward the scoreboard. "We haven't scored since the second-quarter interception. Now we're down 21–17 heading into the fourth quarter. That Eagles defense is tough, and I'd rather see the Bulldogs up this late in the game."

The game continued to be a defensive struggle right up to the two-minute mark. Facing a critical fourth-down decision, the State University Bulldogs were driving into Eagles territory.

All three guys were on their feet, and Matt yelled, "I think they should go for it. They haven't been this close much today!"

More chants came from the crowd: "Goooooo!" rang out in the stands. Matt nodded his head as if they were all in a collective agreement with him.

"I think they should kick a field goal and leave it up to the Kickoff team," Caleb half-joked. Kyle and Matt snapped their heads toward Caleb and noticed his sheepish grin, so neither provided a response.

The Bulldogs' coach opted for a three-point field goal kick. There were some boos from fans who thought the field-goal attempt, even though successful, was a bad call because the Bulldogs were now down by one point with just a little over ninety seconds to play.

On the ensuing kickoff, the Eagles were ready for the onside kick, so the Bulldogs' coach had the kicker send it out of the end zone to put the Eagles on their own twenty-yard line. There were more boos from the stands, and some fans even started to leave.

"You guys want to beat the traffic?" Matt asked.

"A true Bulldog never leaves until there are zeros on the clock," Caleb quipped.

"Not much we can do now," Matt reasoned. "We have only one time-out left. They're just handing the ball off to kill time. If you want to sit in the parking lot for an extra hour, it is fine with me."

Suddenly, the crowd—what was left of it—jumped and cheered. A Bulldogs linebacker had stripped the ball from an Eagles running back who was trying to run out the clock. There was a massive, tangled pileup of players on the field, and both teams were signaling that they had the ball.

"Unbelievable!" shouted Kyle. "I can't believe they didn't just take a knee. Trying to shove it down our throats might have cost them. This is so unbelievable!" Kyle kept his eyes locked on the field.

"That's why you never leave early," Caleb said proudly, feeling as if he'd predicted—or willed—this outcome.

The referees cleared the pile, and a Bulldogs defensive lineman was at the bottom. The lineman was holding tightly onto the ball as if it were the only thing keeping him from spiraling away into outer space. The crowd erupted. All fans were in shock. Bulldogs fans cheered and jumped for joy. Eagles fans stood stunned, knowing they had a much-needed win against the hated Bulldogs within striking distance and might have blown it.

"The Eagles just ripped defeat right out of the jaws of victory. I love it!" Caleb boasted, drawing high fives from Kyle and Matt.

Everyone was on their feet while the Bulldogs ran one running play before calling a time-out, a mere three seconds left on the clock. The Bulldogs' field goal team ran onto the field and lined up.

Kyle felt the tension in his chest, knowing thousands of other fans were feeling the same thing. He had not felt this much suspense since the day he waited for his older brother to walk down the jetway after returning home from war. Yes, Kyle took his football *that* seriously.

As the Bulldogs were ready to snap the ball, the stadium was quiet except for the visitors' section where Eagles fans heckled the kicker. It didn't matter. The kick was up, and it split the uprights. The Bulldogs had just won 23–21 against the loathed Eagles on a cool but sunny November day.

The Scuffle

Kyle, Matt, and Caleb celebrated in the stands and then made their way to the parking lot, feeling energized and pumped. There were hoots and hollers, singing of the Bulldogs fight song, and an overall air of excitement from fans as they hugged and high-fived anyone wearing the red-and-white jersey of the victorious Bulldogs.

Eagles fans, on the flip side, were even more annoyed at this loss than in previous years. They had realistic hopes for a prime-time bowl game. So to see that opportunity slip away after being less than thirty seconds from a victory over the despised Bulldogs, was a bitter pill to swallow.

The wide spectrum of raw emotions seemed to double—even triple—the "normal" amount of brawls as fans made their way out of the stadium to their vehicles or local campus bars. Caleb, Matt, and Kyle managed to steer clear of the fights until they cut through a distant parking lot. There, they saw a group of college-age Eagles fans hounding some elderly Bulldogs fans who had grandchildren in tow.

Kyle was not known to have a temper, but as the kid brother of a US Army Ranger, he had his share of sibling fights (mostly losing them), so he was not afraid to mix it up every now and then. Something about the older couple and their two grandkids getting harassed really bothered Kyle, and that warm sensation of adrenaline overcame him.

"Leave them alone!" Kyle yelled, walking by the group of disgruntled Eagles fans who were leaning on their cars. "*They* didn't fumble the ball for you."

It was like Kyle threw fresh meat to hungry lions. When the Eagles fans saw Kyle, Matt, and Caleb walking by in their red-and-white jerseys, they leaped on them faster than the trio had expected. The four Eagles fans nearest Kyle immediately grabbed him. Four more jumped out of a nearby truck and split up—two attacking Caleb and the other two going after Matt.

This was all going down at the secluded far end of a nearly empty parking lot, with no other Bulldog fans in sight. The guys were outnumbered, but not outmatched, by the Eagles thugs. In the course of the scrap, they threw punches and retreated until Caleb, Matt, and Kyle were all separated from one another in different parts of the parking lot. Caleb landed a punch that knocked the Eagles fan down and then saw his opportunity to get away to a safe area. It took Matt a little longer, but he was chased into another nearby parking lot, where a couple of other Bulldogs fans noticed the fight and came in to break it up.

Kyle was not as fortunate. He got the full force of four guys at once. They dragged him off the parking lot, through some shrubs, and into a small grassy area. Kyle was face down in the grass while they kicked him repeatedly in every part of his body.

A full onslaught of kicks continued for about fifteen seconds even though Kyle felt like it went on forever. Finally, one of the Eagles fans said, "Let's get out of here. This tough guy isn't going anywhere. He's done."

Another thug bent down, and Kyle could smell the stench of stale beer on his breath. The guy said, "But I want to wear a winning jersey home," as he tried to pull the Bulldogs jersey off Kyle.

Before the guy could get the jersey off completely, a shout came from the other side of the shrubs. "Hey, what's going on over there?"

"Nothing, man! Just screwing around with a new friend—that's all." All four offenders walked nonchalantly away from Kyle. It was getting dark out, so the man who yelled didn't see Kyle lying in the shadow of the shrubs.

Meanwhile, Caleb and Matt, after searching for a few minutes, found each other.

"Man, you OK?" Matt, still a little out of breath, asked Caleb.

"Yeah. One got a cheap shot in the back of my head, but I got him back. I'm fine, though. How 'bout you?"

"Not too bad," Matt said, looking at the blood on his elbow and then scanning the parking lot for Kyle. "I'm still trying to figure out what the heck happened. What did Kyle say to set those guys off like that?"

"I just heard him say, 'Leave them alone,' and the next thing I know, in typical Eagles fashion, they jumped us from behind," said Caleb, also surveying the parking lot for Kyle.

"Where's Kyle?" Matt asked.

"I have no idea," Caleb replied.

"Let's split up and look around. Maybe he outran those drunks and is already home. He only lives about a mile away. Otherwise, he would be here, right?" Matt scanned the parking lot again, taking note that only a few cars remained.

"You're probably right," Caleb said. "Not much you can do against four guys other than run, so he might be home by now. It's less than a mile to his house from the stadium."

"You go that way, and I'll go this way," Matt said, pointing in each direction. "Go all the way around, and let's meet back here. I have to get going soon, or Kay will kill me. I have to take her to the airport early tomorrow morning."

Caleb and Matt set off in opposite directions in search of their friend, Kyle.

Kyle, still face down on a small grassy slope a few feet from the shrubs, was in agonizing pain. He felt shooting pains on both sides of his rib cage every time he breathed, so he was pretty sure they were broken. His jaw was sore and his arms and legs throbbed from dozens of kicks. Kyle tried to do a push-up to see where he was and immediately knew it was a bad idea. His wrist hurt so bad that he thought it might also be broken. He bled from his lip and also above his right eye. Kyle, practically shirtless, couldn't move or yell. He wanted to do something but instead lost consciousness.

Matt and Caleb were back at Matt's car. "I didn't see Kyle anywhere. What about you?" Caleb asked, now worried.

"No, I don't think he's here. We would have seen him. Plus, I sent him two texts and tried calling twice—no answer. What do you think?"

"All I know is that he is not here. Let's start heading out. Maybe we'll see him on the way, or he'll call us back, or something." Caleb got into the front passenger seat.

Matt looked around the lot one last time. He even looked straight at the shrubs where Kyle was lying, but he couldn't have spotted him on the other side. "You're right. I've got to drop you off so I can get home, but let's keep looking for him on our way out." Matt started the car and pulled out of the parking lot.

Kyle snapped back to consciousness when he heard his cell phone ringing. The phone was lodged under him, in his front pocket, on the same side as his bad wrist. He figured it was Matt or Caleb calling, but Kyle knew there was no way he was going to get to his phone. Kyle was getting cold, and he started to cough. The pain in his rib cage was so extreme that he let out a quiet moan and passed out again. He regained consciousness and tried to muster up a moan when he heard someone on the nearby sidewalk, but nobody could hear him over the traffic.

Kyle was getting genuinely scared. He thought of his wife, Sarah, at home. They were still practically newlyweds after getting married only twenty months ago. Recently, they both agreed it was time to start adding to their family.

Nearly five years earlier, Kyle's older brother, Rick, was overseas on his second tour of duty with the army.

Sarah also had an older brother who was deployed overseas with the US Air Force. A local support group was holding a Fourth of July event for family members of servicemen and servicewomen serving overseas in the armed forces. Kyle met Sarah for the first time at that event. The feeling in his stomach after meeting her told him she was very different from any other girl he had ever met.

Kyle and Sarah had an immediate bond with family members serving in a combat zone and the constant roller-coaster ride of emotions that was entailed. They also shared an interest in music and sports, although Sarah preferred baseball and golf to Kyle's fanatic love of college basketball and football. They also shared in faith and dedication to family. They fell in love quickly and supported each other in their careers. Sarah finished her MBA and was climbing the ladder with a prominent PR firm while Kyle was a packaging engineer at a local consumer-products manufacturer.

After dating for three years, Kyle decided it was time to pop the question. Of course, it had to be at a football game. Sarah preferred the comfort of her couch and remote control when watching football. So Kyle had to recruit Matt, Caleb, and their girlfriends to coax Sarah out of the house to watch a football game live as a group. Just before the band started playing at halftime, the large digital scoreboard sign flashed this message:

Sarah, you are the MVP in the game of my life, and I never want it to end. Will you marry me?
Kyle

She said yes, and they married six months later.

Kyle started to tear up when he thought of Sarah sitting at home on the couch with her tablet, sipping green tea with her army-logoed blanket on her lap. He was so excited he would be starting a family with Sarah, but knew he could freeze or get pneumonia if nobody found him that night. Kyle closed his eyes and prayed.

The Rescue

Kyle had been lying in the shrubs for nearly an hour when he heard a mother reprimanding her child. A father, mother and their preschool-age child were coming down the sidewalk. The father was a scout for the Bulldogs' next opponent, and he had gotten caught up talking to some other scouts after the game. He knew how big this game was, so he had driven over two hours with his family from a neighboring state, so his three-year-old son could experience his first big college football game. The mother was not as impressed with the last-second win and was getting frustrated at how late they would get home. After getting some grief from his wife, the father walked ahead of her and their child.

Kyle overheard the wife saying, "I have to give him a bath when we get home. You can't stay and talk for hours after games when you bring us with you."

Kyle heard the pitter-patter of small feet stop near the shrubbery. The little boy could see Kyle. "Mama, there's a man lying there. He's naked."

The boy's mother instantly turned around, quickly walking back to where her son stood, and said, "What? Where?" The boy pointed to Kyle.

The mother yelled up to her husband, who was now at least twenty yards ahead. She yelled, "Hon, there's a guy lying in the grass without a shirt. Should we do something?"

"I thought you were in a big hurry, and now you want to stick around and stare at some guy too drunk to walk home after the game? Maybe he'll learn not to get so hammered next time. Come on—let's go," the father yelled back without even breaking stride.

After a short pause, Kyle heard, "Fine, let's go." The mother and son sped up their pace to catch up with the father. Kyle heard their footsteps fade into the distance.

As Kyle stared at the strips of light on the grass that were able to penetrate the wall of shrubs, he could taste the salty, coppery taste in his mouth as his lips continued to bleed. Several spots in both his upper and lower lips were bleeding, making his whole mouth look bloody. He was very cold, especially on his back and stomach, which were exposed to the elements. Kyle guessed the temperature had dropped to around fifty degrees and was even cooler in the grass.

Kyle's phone rang again. He assumed it was his wife, Sarah, calling this time because he never came home this late after a game. He was hoping Matt or Caleb had called his house looking for him because he knew his wife well—she would worry and act quickly to get the campus police involved.

The ringing stopped, and Kyle felt a sense of hopelessness. If he could just get to his phone, he could get some help. Kyle was getting really scared and desperate, so he was able to muster a louder moan when the next group of people strolled by. He caught the attention of some State University students who were walking back to their apartment after celebrating at the campus bars.

Kyle couldn't tell exactly how many there were, but he guessed there would be about four or five of them. He tried to yell for help, but due to the pain in his ribs, it barely came out as an incoherent moan. They heard it. *Surely, they would come over and see that I need help,* Kyle thought. Instead, a male student laughed and said, "Looks like somebody had too much fun at the game today."

Then a female said, "Oh my gosh, his face is bleeding."

Another male said, "That's what happens when you face-plant into the pavement. Looks like he's fallen and can't get up. Loser can't handle his alcohol."

"Are you sure?" asked the same female student. "What if he is hurt or cold?"

"I'm sure he's cold and hurt. You would be, too, if you passed out in a parking lot with no shirt on. Look, it sucks to be this guy, but I need to get back to change and don't have time to do the twelve-step program with this loser. Let's bail."

Another male student said, "Right on. He might even be one of those drunk Eagle fans who got his butt kicked after the game. Serves him right!"

"OK." The female student responded quietly, clearly uncertain about the decision to abandon a bleeding stranger in cold temps regardless of his seemingly inebriated state.

They all walked away, and by now Kyle was so cold he was shivering uncontrollably.

Fortunately, only a few minutes passed before Kyle heard another young man talking on his cell phone. "Like I said, I hate coming here," Kyle heard the man say. "Some stupid fan threw a full water bottle at me after they kicked the winning field goal and hit me right in the nose. It was bleeding so bad I thought it was broke. I've been lying down in the trainer's room for the past hour waiting for it to stop bleeding and the swelling to go down."

The man was almost right next to Kyle when the man stopped and yelled into the phone, "No, it's not broken, but it hurts like heck! How would you like it if—" The man stopped yelling for a few seconds, cut off by the person on the other end of the conversation. "Fine, I'll call you when I get back into town. Should be a little over an hour if I—Hello? Hello? Stupid battery."

Kyle knew he had to do something fast to get this man's attention. He mustered up one good, "Help!" not sure if the man was even still there.

"Hello?" the man said quietly.

When Kyle let out another moan, the man saw him in the grass. He immediately jumped over the shrubs and ran up to Kyle. He said, "Hey, man, you OK?"

Kyle just shook his head back and forth to say no.

The man's name was Jaylen. He was the assistant equipment manager for the Eagles. He was on the team three years ago, and his experiences made him leery of Bulldog fans and their team. Some Bulldog fans could be ruthless to the Eagles players and fans during games, and Jaylen had his share of run-ins with the Bulldogs' faithful. He did not even like to come onto their campus during football season, let alone talk to anyone associated with the Bulldogs.

Jaylen noticed the Bulldogs jersey pushed up to Kyle's neck. After seeing the jersey, Jaylen paused for a second, but he knew a person was hurt and needed help regardless of his favorite team. Jaylen said, "Hang in there, buddy. I'm going to get you some help."

Kyle was relieved. Of course, he was unaware that Jaylen was a former Eagles player; he would not care. Kyle regained hope now that somebody had stopped to help him.

Jaylen pulled out his phone and tried to call 911. "Oh, man, I forgot my battery is dead," Jaylen said. Jaylen started to panic and yelled, "Somebody call nine one one! This man is hurt." Some people on the other side of the parking lot stopped to look but couldn't make out what he was yelling, so they just kept walking.

Jaylen took off his coat and put it over Kyle. He actually felt sorry for this Bulldog fan who'd taken a nasty beating. Jaylen said, "Not sure what happened here, but I think I'm going to have to get you to the hospital myself. Can you walk at all?"

Kyle could only whisper. "I don't know. I am so cold, so let's try."

Jaylen clapped his hands together and said, "OK, here's what we're going to do. I'm going to pull my car as close as I can and get you inside. Once you're in, I'll take you to the ER. Sound good?" Kyle thought Jaylen sounded like he was calling a football play rather than trying to help a badly beaten man. Still, he gave Jaylen a thumbs-up.

"Good. I'll be back in about two minutes. Don't go anywhere," Jaylen caught himself just as those last words came out and looked to see Kyle's reaction. Kyle gave a half smile and another thumbs-up.

A few minutes later, Jaylen was pulling into the parking lot, just to the other side of the shrubs. He jumped out and opened the back door of his four-door sedan. He ran over to Kyle and said, "You ready for this?"

Kyle nodded his head yes, and Jaylen bent down to put Kyle's arm around him. Jaylen tried to straighten up slowly, but Kyle—at nearly two hundred pounds—was just too heavy. Jaylen got down on his knees, as low as he could, and put Kyle's arm around him, again. He stood up, one leg at a time. *All those days in the gym are really paying off now,* Jaylen thought.

Kyle groaned loudly, the pain in his ribs and wrist almost unbearable. Jaylen asked while he was walking Kyle to his car, "Do you want me to put you down?"

Kyle responded in his loudest voice yet, "No, just get me to the ER no matter what!"

Jaylen smiled and said, "You've got it." He walked Kyle to the car and lowered him into the backseat. He laid Kyle across the seat and then ran around to the driver's seat. Jaylen looked back and told Kyle, "Just relax. I'll get you to the ER as fast as I can."

Kyle was motionless as he looked up and out the window, watching the streetlights and an occasional tree pass him by. There was a sense of calmness about him now that he was safe and en route to the ER.

Jaylen pulled in front of the ER entrance, ran inside, and came back with an emergency medical technician (EMT) to check on Kyle in the backseat.

The EMT said, "Sir, can you hear me? Can you talk?"

Kyle whispered, "Yes. I think my ribs are broken, and it is hard to breathe and talk."

"OK, we're going to get you inside." The EMT raced back to get a gurney and three more people to help get Kyle inside the hospital.

After a nurse examined Kyle's wounds, took his vital signs, and began treatment, she turned to Jaylen. "Is he a friend of yours?"

"No, not really," said Jaylen. "I just heard him calling for help, so I brought him here."

"He's lucky you did," said the nurse, checking the IV line. "He's in pretty bad shape and might not have fared too well in this cold. I'm sure he appreciates your help."

The nurse turned to Kyle and asked, "Is there someone we can call? A family member or a close friend?"

By now, Kyle's pain meds were kicking in, and he softly said, "In my front pocket of my pants, over there. Look up Sarah, my wife, and call her. Tell her I'm here, and she will come right down."

The nurse looked up at Jaylen and said, "Go ahead, and call her please."

Jaylen was a little shocked and uncomfortable about calling a stranger's wife to tell her that her husband was in the hospital, but he did as the nurse told him. He found Sarah's number and called. After one ring, she answered, "Kyle, are you OK? Where are you?"

Jaylen took a deep breath and said, "Sarah, Kyle is in the ER at Mercy Medical. He is a little banged up but will be OK. He wants you to come down here as soon as you can."

Sarah was quiet at the end of the phone. Jaylen could tell she was crying when she said, "Can I talk to him?"

"He has some broken ribs, so it's hard for him to talk, but I'll give him the phone."

Kyle whispered a couple of sentences to Sarah and then hung up. The medical staff went back and forth into the room, which was generally quiet as Kyle and Jaylen watched about ten minutes of an old episode of *Friends* on the flat-screen television mounted to the wall.

Jaylen was anxious to get out of the ER. He'd spent some time in there when he tore ligaments in his knee and just wanted to get back home. Jaylen stood up and said, "Take care, buddy. Hope you get well soon."

Kyle grabbed Jaylen's arm and said, "I can't thank you enough for saving me. Really, thank you so much. I'm so grateful."

A doctor and a different nurse walked in and asked Jaylen, "What happened here?"

"I don't know. I just found him this way and knew he needed some help," Jaylen said, recounting the scene.

Sarah ran in a few moments later and gently hugged Kyle. She was crying but collected herself as Kyle briefly whispered the details after the game. She pushed back his brown hair and kissed his forehead as he started to drift asleep from the pain medications.

Again, Jaylen moved toward the door, but Sarah stopped him. She was smiling now and said, "Kyle says you saved him. Thank you so much for bringing him here. He says he lost Matt and Caleb. Where are they?"

Jaylen replied, "I don't know who Matt and Caleb are. I just did what others would do if they saw somebody who needed help."

Looking a little confused, Sarah asked, "How do you know my husband? How did you find him?"

"I don't know your husband," Jaylen said, looking Sarah in the eye. "I was leaving the game late because I was on the Eagles sideline and a Bulldog fan hit me in the nose with a water bottle. I thought I broke my nose, so I stayed in the trainer's room for some treatment. When I finally left to go back to my car, I heard your husband yell for help."

It was almost as if Sarah only heard one word that Jaylen said because she responded, "You are with the Eagles?"

"Yes, ma'am," Jaylen said proudly. "I was on the team for two years, and I graduated three years ago. Now I'm their assistant equipment manager."

Sarah turned a little pale when she heard that. She asked, "Why did you stop when so many others must have just walked by?"

Jaylen paused for a second, looked down and then back up, and then said, "I'm sure others would have helped if they'd seen him. During the game, we're Eagles and Bulldogs, but at the end of the day, we are all people. We're all God's children, so that makes you and your husband—and everyone else in that stadium—my neighbor. Neighbors help neighbors, no matter what!"

Sarah smiled and responded, "So true. God bless you."

Sarah thanked Jaylen again as he left the hospital. Then, she went back to Kyle and stayed by his side until he was discharged from the hospital.

Overview

This story is a modern retelling of the parable of the Good Samaritan in Luke 10:25–37.

In this contemporary version of the story, Kyle is the man walking to Jericho that was beaten. The family with the toddler and the college students are the people you would have expected to stop and offer help. Jaylen is the Good Samaritan that stopped and helped an enemy. As represented in both instances, the parable demonstrates that we are all neighbors. We should love, help, and care for *all* people!

Moral of the Story: Each man, woman, and child is your neighbor. Always help a neighbor in need!

Did you know?

The reason Jesus told this story in Luke 10:25–37 was to answer a question asked by someone in the crowd. Jesus told the people that the most important thing was to love God first and then love your neighbor. Someone in the crowd asked, "Who is our neighbor?" Jesus told them the parable of the Good Samaritan, which is one of the most well-known stories in the Bible. Now we know that every person is our neighbor.

ONE IN A HUNDRED

Small explosions rattled the windows, and white smoke partially filled the room. Even as the red lava oozed off the side of the volcano, nobody moved. Mrs. Natalie Parker's science class was conducting their annual volcano experiment, and this year, it was epic. Her class spent days perfecting the volcano and the eruptions that were designed to teach them about the earth's active core as they studied earth science.

Shouts of "Whoa," "Awesome," and "More lava" rang out from the classroom.

Mr. Meyers knocked and immediately stuck his head inside her classroom. He said, "Excuse me, Mrs. Parker. We're having a math test next door; so could you please lower the volume on the eruptions a bit?"

"I'm sorry, Mr. Meyers. My students maybe did too good of a job creating a volcano this year. We will keep it down."

Mrs. Parker convinced her class to keep the volume down to a low roar. They continued to experiment with volcanic eruptions until class was nearly over.

"We're almost out of time, so I need everyone to clean up your areas and yourselves. Once you're done, please begin reading chapter 8 in your science book until the bell rings."

Mrs. Parker loved her students as much as she loved teaching. She had taught at Grace Community Charter School (GCCS) almost her entire career since graduating from college. She earned her degree in elementary education nine years earlier. Natalie Parker was unsure of exactly which grade or specialty field she wanted to pursue right after graduation. She had several jobs before her current position. Her first job was at a local day-care chain, and she quickly realized that was not her passion. After less than a year at the day-care company, she took a job at GCCS as a teacher's aide. Natalie was very organized and an avid reader, both of which led her to become the school's librarian in her second year. In her fourth year, she became a first-grade teacher. Natalie loved the first graders. Nevertheless, she jumped at the opportunity to become the first full-time science teacher for all of the students in the fifth through eighth grades at GCCS. Now, at age twenty-nine, with two years under her belt as the science teacher, Natalie loved teaching each and every day.

Forty-five minutes after the school day was over and the last students had left for the day, Natalie packed up her bag and prepared to go home. On her way to the parking lot, she stopped by Mrs. Simpson's sixth-grade classroom.

"I hope we didn't bother you today," Natalie stated as she stopped at the classroom door.

"No, not at all, but I heard Mr. Meyers took you behind the woodshed for a good whipping."

"Hardly a whipping, but he did stop by, so I felt bad that I disturbed his math test. He gets so uptight when he's teaching his junior-high students how to divide the fractions of the square root of pi."

Both women laughed, and then Mrs. Simpson asked, "Are you and Keith going out to the lake this weekend? I think Justin and I are going to head out there, and it would be great if you two could come."

"Which day are you going?"

"Justin has plans on Saturday, so we'll probably go on Sunday," Mrs. Simpson replied.

"That sounds like fun, but I'm teaching Sunday school, so we can't make it on Sunday. Maybe another time."

"Wow, you're a saint, Natalie. I couldn't give up every Sunday after dealing with this all week. I don't know how you do it."

"I just love teaching those students. They're at such a fun age, and they soak up everything you teach them. Anyway, Keith and I have plans tonight, so I need to head home now. I'll see you tomorrow. Bye," Natalie said as she left the classroom and went home.

A Full Flock

A couple of weeks later, Natalie was teaching a class of sixth graders about the biology of plants. She was explaining germination and asked the class, "New plants sprout from seeds, so where do the seeds come from?"

"Their mommy," rang out an answer from the front row to some laughter.

Natalie sternly replied, "Logan, what did I tell you about yelling out answers without raising your hand? You are not too far off, so consider this your warning today."

"Now, does anyone else have a serious answer? Please raise your hands."

Several students raised their hands. Natalie noticed a student new to GCCS, who did not raise her hand much, so Natalie called on her.

"Olivia, do you know the answer?"

"God made the seeds."

A few students snickered, and Natalie was a little shocked to hear that answer, so she asked, "Are you trying to be funny, or is that your honest answer?"

"Well, I know that plants make seeds to make other plants, but my grandma always taught me everything in nature comes from God."

"Olivia, you're right—plants produce seeds that are carried by the wind and birds and are spread on the ground in order to produce new plants. Could you please see me after class?" Natalie stated as she walked back to her desk to collect her thoughts and turn to the next page of their science book.

Olivia looked scared and did not raise her hand the rest of the hour. This was her first year at GCCS, and she appeared to have a couple of friends. Olivia was a quiet student. Natalie was concerned about her and wanted to get to know her a little better.

After class, Olivia shuffled slowly up to Natalie's desk when all of the other students had left.

Natalie started, "How are you liking Grace Community School?"

"It's OK."

"It looks like you have a few new friends. Is everyone nice to you?"

"Yes."

Natalie could see Olivia was either very shy or perhaps even a little intimidated by her. Natalie was just under five foot ten, and she cleared six feet when she wore heels. She had played on the basketball team in high school and maintained her athletic physique. Her naturally curly, shoulder-length, brown hair made her seem even taller, which was intimidating to some of the students. Natalie chose to move past the small talk and be direct with her next question.

"When you said God makes the seeds, were you trying to be funny, or were you being serious?"

"Serious."

"Did your parents teach you that, or did you learn it at church?"

"My parents don't go to church. When my grandma was still alive, she read the Bible every day. She taught me all about God and Jesus."

"Honey, I'm sorry about your grandma. When did she pass away?"

"Last year," Olivia said while looking down at the floor.

Natalie's heart sank for Olivia. It was obvious she really missed her grandma and everything she taught her. Without giving it too much thought, Natalie blurted out, "If your parents can take you to church, I also teach Sunday school if you want to keep learning about Jesus."

Olivia looked up, smiled, and said, "OK."

Natalie explained where the church was and what time it started and wrote a note for Olivia so she could go to her next class a few minutes late. Natalie felt bad for the pain Olivia was feeling with the loss of her grandma but also felt good for reaching out to her and inviting her to church. *Perhaps that would help Olivia feel a connection with her grandma,* she thought.

Later that evening, Natalie was still feeling good about the invitation she extended to Olivia. She told her husband, Keith, about it while he was working in the garage. Natalie could not tell if he was paying attention, but he said he thought it sounded great. So Natalie was happy with that answer and changed the subject. She still had a positive feeling about her outreach to Olivia until after third period the next day. She had an open period for prep, and the math teacher next door, Mr. Meyers, popped into her classroom with some bad news.

"Hey, Natalie. You have to be careful with the students."

Natalie was confused and instantly defensive. She was not sure if it was the smug look on Mr. Meyers's face as he looked down at Natalie over his reading glasses or the bluntness of his entry. Natalie snapped back, "What do you mean?"

"Olivia's brother, Marco, was in my class when he saw her walking in the hallway five minutes after she was supposed to be in class. After class had ended, he stopped her outside my door and asked her why she was late. I overheard her say that you asked her to go to church. I also heard Marco say that Mom and Dad were not going to be happy, and then they both walked to their next class."

Natalie instantly felt a pit in her stomach. She knew better but had wanted to help Olivia so badly that she might have crossed the line by inviting her to church.

GCCS was a public school, and she could be in hot water if Olivia's parents were upset.

"That's not good," Natalie slowly stated.

"You know, I don't have any problems with it, but this is a public school, and you know how big of a fight Mr. Ellis had with a few parents just over the word *grace* in the school's name. Fortunately for Mr. Ellis, his daughter is named Grace, or we might be working for a school with a different name. You and I both know why he really named this school Grace, but that's not the point. Some parents don't want religion of any type associated with the school, so you can't invite students you barely know to church."

"I know! I know! Thanks for telling me, but I have a lot of work to do, so we'll have to talk about this later." Natalie flipped open a book on her desk, and Mr. Meyers left the room. She was mad at herself for letting this happen and was concerned that Olivia's parents would complain to the school.

Natalie made it through the rest of the day but could not get the situation with Olivia off her mind. Natalie texted her husband, Keith, that she was having a bad day, so he cooked her favorite dinner—shrimp pasta primavera without mushrooms. During dinner, Keith noticed she was quieter than normal and asked, "What's wrong? You've barely touched your food."

"I'm sorry. It's delicious. I made a mistake at school, and I can't stop thinking about it."

"What happened?"

"Remember that girl I told you about yesterday? The one who lost her grandma so I invited her to come to church?"

"Was I working on the Camaro? I guess I wasn't really paying attention. What happened, again?"

Natalie loved Keith with all her heart, but sometimes she wondered if he loved his car more. Keith is in sales, and he has been selling food and supplies to restaurants since he graduated from college. The entire time he saved up to buy and restore his dream 1969 Chevy Camaro. Last year his dream came true. He had been in the garage as often as possible restoring his baby ever since. Keith had also been in the doghouse often for spending too much time working on the Camaro.

"Keith, this is what I'm talking about. This is important, and you can't even stop working on the car for a second to listen to me."

"I'm sorry," Keith replied sincerely.

"OK. I have a student who used to always read the Bible with her grandma until she passed away last year, and her parents don't go to church. She really wants to have a connection with God, so I invited her to our church."

"Babe, you know you can't do that. Even if you know it's the right thing to do; her parents may not agree."

"I know, and that's what's bothering me. I know I shouldn't have done it, but I don't regret it. I believe it was the right thing to do for her," Natalie said as she took her dish to the sink.

Still facing the sink while looking out the window, she said, "Keith, you know I have to do what's right. As the daughter of a pastor, I've seen it all my life. I saw my parents live it, and my brother and sister are the same way today, too. Sometimes, doing the right thing can also have consequences, but that's all I know. I believe I did the right thing for Olivia."

She turned around to face Keith. "What are you thinking?"

"Well, if it doesn't work out, you can always be my assistant and schlep pork loins, tin foil, and cans of diced tomatoes with me," Keith said with a smile. He put his hands in front of his face, pretending to block a potential punch or dish thrown his way.

"Go work on your car. I'm going to bed early tonight."

Keith walked over and kissed her on the cheek, "You know I'll support you, no matter what. If you believe it's the right thing to do, then I'm in your corner. Good night."

Natalie went to their bedroom, crawled into bed, and prayed. She prayed Olivia would be able to keep her relationship with God.

For the next couple of weeks at school, Natalie never said anything to Olivia about church or the previous conversation. The principal never called Natalie into her office nor did she receive any e-mails or phone calls from Olivia's parents. She figured either they did not find out, or they were not upset.

That Sunday, Natalie was in front of the room talking to some students just before her Sunday school class in the youth ministry building at her church. As the last students were coming through the door, she noticed the woman from Guest Services bringing a new girl into the room. The girl looked very familiar—it was Olivia. Natalie was so happy to see her that she almost ran over to hug her, but instead, she just waved and smiled so Olivia would not feel too uncomfortable.

Olivia took her seat in the back. Natalie began with a prayer followed by the lesson that day on Joseph from the book of Genesis. She talked about how Joseph was his father's favorite son and how his jealous brothers sold him into slavery. Joseph was also imprisoned before he explained the meaning of a dream to the king and became the king's aid. Eventually, Joseph's brothers who beat and sold him would come to Egypt and bow down to him. Natalie told the class that despite his tumultuous life, Joseph always had God by his side during good and bad times. She saw Olivia crack a small smile. Natalie knew Olivia was getting the information and inspiration that she needed.

After class, Natalie approached Olivia and asked her, "Did your parents bring you?"

"Yeah, my dad dropped me off."

"That's great. I am so happy they are OK with you coming to church."

"They're not really happy about it, but they think it will help me feel better about my grandma. So they said they would bring me once in a while."

"That's a great start! I hope I get to see you here more often."

Several months passed, and Olivia came to church almost every Sunday. Natalie noticed that she was really growing at both church and school. Olivia was becoming more social with the other girls at school, and she was participating in the small group sessions at church. Natalie was proud of herself for reaching out to Olivia.

The school year was coming to an end, and Natalie's church always had baptisms just before summer break. Natalie made the announcement to the students about baptism. She told them they should talk it over with their parents if they were ready to say yes to Jesus. After class, Olivia approached Natalie and said, "I think I want to be baptized, Mrs. Parker."

"That's great. You should talk to your parents about it because it is a big decision."

"I know. I don't know if they'll like it."

"I'm sure they'll support it if you want to do it. They have been bringing you to church for months now, so they must be OK with it—right?

"I guess."

Natalie was sure Olivia's parents would approve. They did not complain about Natalie asking her to church while at school, and they had dropped her off at church for several months now. Natalie could not imagine her parents disapproving.

Next Sunday, Natalie prepared to answer questions on baptism and get a head count on the number of students who wanted to get baptized. She noticed that Olivia did not show up that week but dismissed it as a coincidence.

A few more weeks passed, and Olivia did not show up to Sunday school. Natalie did not dare discuss it while at GCCS even though she had Olivia in class four days a week. She was dying to know why Olivia stopped coming on Sundays.

GCCS finally entered the last week of school before summer break. Olivia missed the baptism, and Natalie *had* to know why. On the last day of school, she stopped Olivia after class and asked her why she stopped coming to church on Sundays.

"I asked my parents about baptism, and they said no. They said I had enough, and now it was going too far. They won't take me anymore on Sunday," Olivia replied.

"What? I'm sorry Olivia. I thought for sure they would say yes. I'm so sorry."

"That's OK."

"Can I call them and see if they'll change their minds?"

"No, I don't think that's a good idea. They were pretty mad."

"I'm sorry Olivia. You have a great summer, and I look forward to seeing you next school year!"

Natalie gave Olivia a half hug, and Olivia was off for the summer.

Later that evening, Natalie and her husband were dining out to celebrate the end of the school year. This was typically a joyous time for Natalie and her fellow teachers. In the summer, they had more time to spend with their families and enjoy the outdoors. Natalie and Keith spent most of their free time towing both of their personal watercraft to one of the many lakes in the area. They both loved summer.

The server placed two glasses of red wine on the table. Keith grabbed his glass and raised it. "To summer."

"To summer." Natalie toasted Keith back.

They completed their dinner. While they waited for the check, Keith noticed Natalie was a little distant and asked, "Honey, is everything OK? You're usually on cloud nine this time of the year."

"I'm excited about the summer, but I'm concerned for Olivia—that GCCS student who was also coming to church for a few months."

"I remember. Whatever happened to her?"

Natalie explained the entire situation. After she had finished, they paid the bill and drove home. During the ride home, Keith told Natalie, "I hate to see you down like this. Olivia will be OK. You have a lot of students, so don't risk your job for that one student."

"Why would you say that?" Natalie replied, starting to get angry.

"Because I know how you are. You get your mind set on something, and you don't give up until you get it. Can't you just focus on all the other students who love and depend on you?"

Natalie was looking out the window as if the pasture they were passing was the most interesting thing on the planet. She never responded and neither said a word the rest of the drive home.

Later that month, Natalie and Keith were spending a Saturday on a friend's boat. Justin and Kim Simpson had been friends with Natalie and Keith since Natalie started teaching at GCCS, where Kim was the veteran sixth-grade teacher. Kim Simpson had two grown boys and had been teaching for over twenty years. So Natalie often went to her for advice on teaching and life.

While docked near one of the lake's sandy beaches, Kim and Natalie reclined in the front of the boat. They watched the other families enjoy the warm weather and the cool water. Kim turned to Natalie and asked, "How is your summer going?"

"Pretty good. How about yours?"

"Too fast. I'm going to miss days like this, but it's always good to get back to school. You seem a little preoccupied lately. What's going on?"

"It's that girl, Olivia. I felt I was helping her, but her parents just yanked her out of my Sunday school class. I keep wondering if I should do something."

"I have two words for you," Kim stated as she propped up on one elbow and faced Natalie. "Don't do it."

"That's three words."

"Now you know why I'm stuck in sixth grade," Kim said, laughing.

"Funny, Kim, but I'm serious."

"So am I. As a parent, I can tell you that you don't want someone else pushing anything on one of your kids that you don't support. Not everyone understands or agrees with everything we do in our personal lives. Just focus on all the other students who you are helping."

"I keep hearing that, but it doesn't help. I understand what you're saying, and I appreciate it," Natalie said while cracking a forced, fake smile. She wanted to change the subject, so she suggested a race on the personal watercraft against Justin or Keith, which was like offering candy to a kindergarten student. They could not resist, so Natalie quickly hopped off the boat and onto her watercraft. She never mentioned Olivia again the rest of the day.

One rainy morning, Natalie was looking out the window while sipping her morning coffee. Her plans for the lake were canceled, so her mind began to drift to Olivia again. Natalie felt she could persuade Olivia's parents if she could only explain how much Sunday school was helping Olivia.

Natalie found Olivia's phone number in the student roster and put it in her cell phone. Several times that day, she would scroll through her contact list until she landed on Olivia's number. Then one time, she hit Send.

Natalie was not exactly sure what she would say when someone answered, but the urge to do something was too great. The phone rang three times, and Natalie considered hanging up, but she couldn't. She had to convince Olivia's parents. After the fourth ring, the voice mail started. It was Olivia's mom. While the greeting was playing, Natalie had dozens of ideas running through her head until she heard the beep. After a couple of seconds of silence, Natalie took a deep breath. Then, she spilled everything on her mind onto the voice mail for the next forty-five seconds. She explained how much Olivia was thriving in Sunday school, how she seemed to be coping better with the loss of her grandma, and how she was making more friends at school. Finally, Natalie hit the End Call button and collapsed into the family-room couch. She smiled while replaying her message in her head because Natalie thought it was compelling. She was confident that Olivia's parents would see the benefits and bring her back to Sunday school.

A Sheep Is Lost

Natalie was in her classroom often the rest of the summer as she prepared for the upcoming year. She never saw or heard from Olivia's mom. Meet-the-Teacher night finally arrived to kick off the new school year. Natalie loved meeting all of her new students and was excited to talk about the scientific projects with the parents.

Meet-the-Teacher night was almost over, and Natalie noticed that neither Olivia nor her parents came into her room. Natalie was a little worried that Olivia's parents did not feel comfortable coming into her classroom, so she walked over to Mr. Meyers's room to see if he saw them.

"How was tonight?" Natalie forced out some small talk before she would reveal her real reason for stopping by.

"Pretty good. There are a lot of familiar faces and a few new students. I think this is going to be a good year," Mr. Meyers replied.

"Speaking of familiar faces, I didn't see Olivia or her parents in my classroom. Did you?"

"I didn't see Olivia, but her older brother, Marco, was here with his mom. At some point, I asked Marco if Olivia was with her dad, and he said she was going to a new school this year."

"What? Why?" Natalie snapped back almost yelling.

"I don't know. I didn't ask."

Natalie began to feel nauseous, so she walked quickly to the nearest bathroom. She went into a stall and started to cry. Natalie felt horrible for the pain she caused Olivia, and now she was going to a new school because of the voice mail.

After a couple of minutes, Natalie's sadness and guilt turned to anger. *How could Olivia's parents not see that I was only trying to help her,* Natalie thought as she splashed cold water on her face. She composed herself and went back to her classroom to complete the Meet-the-Teacher night.

Natalie drove home and burst into the garage where Keith was working on his car. "Guess what?" Natalie yelled, a little out of breath. Keith immediately knew something was wrong, so he stopped what he was doing and came over to Natalie. He could tell she had been crying.

"What happened?"

"Olivia's parents are pulling her from Grace Community School. They don't want her by me because I invited her to church. I can't believe it. I'm livid right now."

Keith did not offer a response. He stood silently looking Natalie right in her bloodshot, green eyes. After several seconds of silence, Natalie spoke first. "Aren't you going to say something?"

"When are you going to go after her?"

"What do you mean?"

"Natalie, I know you, and I know how important this girl is to you. You have to do what you think is right because that's what you do. I'm not crazy about you potentially getting fired over this, especially since you are such a skilled, passionate, and caring teacher. But you are an even better person, so I will support you no matter what happens. Just be careful."

The support from Keith is just what Natalie needed. She hugged him and said, "Thanks. I will be careful."

Natalie decided she needed to speak with Olivia's mom and dad face to face. She felt that was the only way she could convince them that Sunday school was helping Olivia. She looked up Olivia's home address and committed to going to her home the coming weekend so she could speak with Olivia's parents in person.

The Search

Natalie woke up the next Saturday morning earlier than normal. She knew today was the day she would visit Olivia's house, and she could not stop thinking about all the things she wanted to say. She was not sure how Olivia's parents would react, so Natalie tried to picture all of the possible scenarios in her head in order to be prepared.

A little after nine, Natalie decided she would drive herself crazy thinking about all the possibilities that could occur during her visit with Olivia's parents. She showered, put on makeup, and picked up some coffee at her favorite coffee shop as she drove across town to Olivia's house. Natalie did not even notice her favorite song was playing on the radio. She was focused on the talk with Olivia's parents.

Natalie pulled up in front of the modest, brick bungalow home that matched Olivia's address and parked on the other side of the street. She double-checked the address and turned off the car without turning away from the house. After a deep breath, she began walking up the sidewalk to Olivia's house.

Once she was on the porch, she felt like her shoes were made of lead because each step was more and more difficult. She got to the door, and mild panic began. She stared at the door but was too scared to knock. Natalie began to convince herself this was a bad idea and considered turning around and leaving as she heard a male yell on the other side of the door: "Mom, have you seen my new controller? I can't play this game without it." He sounded like he was right on the other side of the door, and Natalie did not want to get caught just standing there, so she quickly rang the doorbell. Olivia's older brother, Marco, answered the door while Olivia was coming down the hallway.

Natalie was not sure Marco recognized her outside of school, so she introduced herself. "Hi, I am Mrs. Parker from Grace Community Charter School. Are your mom and dad home? I would like to speak with them."

Natalie noticed the fear in Olivia's face and started to get even more nervous.

"My dad is at work, but my mom is home. Mom! Somebody is at the door for you," Marco yelled and walked away, leaving the door wide open.

A few seconds later, a woman appeared at the door. She looked like a taller, older version of Olivia with her brown eyes and curly black hair. Natalie was sure it was her mom.

"Hi. I'm Mrs. Parker. I was Olivia's teacher at Grace Community Charter School and at Sunday school. It's nice to meet you."

"Hi. I'm Teresa. I'm Olivia and Marco's mom. I'm not sure who has been told at Grace Community School, but Olivia is going to a new school this year."

"I know; that's why I'm here," Natalie replied quickly. "Can I come in and talk to you for a few minutes?"

"Um, the place is a mess, and I wasn't expecting anyone today. Can we just talk here?"

"I would really like to speak with you inside," Natalie said with the biggest smile she could muster.

"OK. Please give me a minute."

Teresa walked into the hallway. She yelled for Marco and Olivia to go to the family room to watch TV while she talked to Mrs. Parker. Teresa came back and said, "Come in."

Natalie followed Teresa into the kitchen.

Teresa cleared some piles of mail and papers off the kitchen table before pulling out a chair for Natalie. Teresa offered Natalie something to drink, and Natalie complimented her on how well she decorated the kitchen. Teresa explained this was their first home after renting for many years and maintaining an older home was a challenge but one she enjoyed. After nearly five minutes of small talk, Teresa asked, "So what brings you to our house on a Saturday morning?"

"I'm sorry just to show up unannounced, but I wanted to talk to you about something that I think is best to discuss live."

"OK."

"Did you get my voice mail a couple of months ago?"

"I did, but I didn't think it warranted a reply. My husband and I made the decision to put Olivia in a new school that we feel better suits her needs."

Natalie leaned forward and said, "I understand, but I was hoping you could let Olivia come back to Sunday school again."

Teresa shuffled a bit in her chair and said, "I'm sorry Mrs. Parker, but we don't believe in organized religion. I rarely went to church growing up, and my husband stopped going while he was a teenager. We appreciate all you've done for Olivia, but we're trying to prepare her for the real world, and Sunday school isn't something we feel is necessary for Olivia."

"But if you—" Natalie began to explain, but Teresa was starting to get upset and cut her off.

"Just a minute, Mrs. Parker. We've been very patient and understanding with you and your beliefs, so I hope you'll be respectful of ours. My husband was willing to let Olivia try it for a while, but then she started talking about how we all should consider getting saved, and then she wanted to get baptized. He saw a lot of things at church he didn't like when he was growing up, and he doesn't want his kids to go through that."

Natalie could see Teresa was upset and that she was not going to win her over today at her kitchen table. Teresa's husband had a negative experience at his church, and they were just trying to protect their kids.

"I'm not here to upset you, so I apologize if I did. I just wanted you to know how much I appreciated having Olivia in my classes. Thank you for letting me come in, so I could speak with you. I really appreciate your time," Natalie said as she stood up and began walking to the front door with Teresa walking closely behind her.

"I do have one quick question for you before I go. Did you see any positive changes in Olivia when she was going to Sunday school? Did she seem to be coping with the loss of her grandma better? Did she seem a little more outgoing?

Teresa appeared caught off guard by those questions. She responded, "Um, yeah. She has been doing better coping with the death of her grandmother—my husband's mother—but I imagine the passing time helped heal her wounds as much as anything at Sunday school."

"That's not completely true," Natalie said confidently. "Time does not heal wounds, hope does. Olivia had learned about Jesus, love, redemption, and eternal life from her grandma. She believes she'll be with her grandma in Heaven again someday. In Sunday school, she learned that Jesus died for her and that He loves her just the way she is. She was happier because she has hope!"

Teresa looked down and said, "Maybe she does."

Once Natalie was on the front porch, she said, "I know Olivia will do great at whatever school you choose for her to attend. My only hope is that she can come back to Sunday school. I think it's the best thing for her. Thanks again for allowing me to come in and talk to you today." She turned around and walked back to her car.

Natalie drove back home feeling confident that Teresa would at least consider Sunday school again. When she arrived home, Keith was waiting in the front yard. "How did it go?"

"She let me in, and I got to tell her why I thought it was so important. So I guess it went as well as it could."

"You're not going to let this go, are you?"

"Nope," Natalie said as she walked past Keith into the house with a big smile.

A month later, Natalie was preparing the room for the next Sunday school class. She expected Olivia would have come back by now, so Natalie was growing less confident she would ever come back. Natalie opened class in prayer and turned off the lights to show a short video on forgiveness. When a student turned the lights back on, Natalie noticed a student standing in the back of the room.

It was Olivia, and this time, Natalie did not hold back her emotions. She ran up to Olivia, hugged her, and led her to a seat in the front of the class. Still smiling profusely, Natalie composed herself and told the class she felt the need to read a passage from Luke 15:3–6. It was about the one sheep out of a flock of one hundred that was lost and that the shepherd went looking for it.

Then Jesus told them this parable: "Suppose one of you has a hundred sheep and loses one of them. Doesn't he leave the ninety-nine in the open country and go after the lost sheep until he finds it? And when he finds it, he joyfully puts it on his shoulders and goes home. Then he calls his friends and neighbors together and says, 'Rejoice with me; I have found my lost sheep.'"

After class was over and all the other students left, Natalie sat down next to Olivia. "I'm so happy you came back. Did your dad bring you again?"

"No, my mom brought me this time."

"Really? That's great news. She seemed one hundred percent against it when we talked."

"I know. I prayed to God that my mom would understand, and I told her that Jesus gives me hope." Natalie noticed a sparkle in Olivia's beautiful brown eyes when she spoke.

Natalie was so proud of Olivia that she hugged her again and said, "Anything is possible with God."

"I know. My mom said she may have some questions for me after Sunday school, so I think God is working on her, too."

"Wow! That's great, Olivia."

"I know. My mom is waiting for me now, so I have to go. Bye, Mrs. Parker."

Olivia ran to her mom's car, and together they talked about the lost sheep story on the way home.

Overview

This story is the modern rendition of the parable about the shepherd who left his flock of ninety-nine sheep to find one missing sheep, in Luke 15:1–7.

Here, Natalie takes the role of the shepherd, and Olivia is the lost sheep. Although we never learn about her sin in the story, we know Olivia is a sinner because she is human. This parable was told by Jesus to the high priests to demonstrate that *all* people, including sinners, are important to God and that He will rejoice when any person who loses his or her way repents and comes back to the flock.

Moral of the Story: Jesus loves you right where you are, no matter what you have done. God wants us in His family, and He may even pursue some of us. We just need to accept Him and join the family!

THE BAD COP

"After tying him up on top of the wood altar he'd built, he pulled out his knife, prepared to take the life of his one and only son!" the dean of religious studies, Simon Clarke, roared, pacing in front of the class. "As you all know, God stopped Abraham and spared his son, Isaac, with an alternative sacrifice. That, ladies and gentlemen, is the ultimate display of obedience and trust in God that we should all strive to achieve." Dean Clarke stopped center stage and faced his audience of freshman students.

"Your assignment is to read the next chapter on Isaac and Ishmael and come prepared to discuss the deeds, direction, and descendants of each. Class is dismissed. I will see you all again on Thursday." Dean Clarke shut the cover of his tablet and walked off the stage.

Dean Simon Clarke was a firebrand instructor and recent dean at Southern Christian University (SCU). SCU was known for having some of the brightest students and most intelligent instructors in the region, and Dean Clarke always landed near the top of the list of experts in his field.

Over sixteen years ago, Dean Clarke started out on the fast track at SCU as a student. He graduated from the prestigious school with a master's degree in religious instruction and Ph.D. in theology. Now as the dean of religious studies, he insisted on teaching one required freshman course "to ensure that all students have the proper foundation to succeed at Southern Christian University."

Dean Clarke and his young wife, Tiffany, were both active in the community. They were respected among the local political and business leaders. Dean Clarke was a pretty important guy in the small college town that hosted SCU, and he knew it.

Tiffany greeted her husband when he arrived home after class. She wore a big smile on her face and held a letter in her hand. "Simon, I opened the mail you told me to, and guess who was asked to be the keynote speaker at the mayor's Sixth Annual Prayer Dinner next month?"

"I assume that would be me," Dean Clarke responded, seemingly uninterested as he flipped through the rest of the mail on the counter.

"Why aren't you excited? This is a big deal. It's one of the biggest events of the year, and everyone will be there. I'm excited for you." Tiffany responded with surprise.

"Yes, you're right. It is a big deal, and I am excited they chose me," Simon said, planting a kiss on his wife's cheek. "It's just that I fought so long and hard to get prayer back into this town, and this event always reminds me of the people who tried to derail my plans. So it doesn't feel as joyous as it should."

Tiffany put the mail down and looked up into her husband's eyes. "That's one of the things I really love about you—your drive and determination to do what's right. So if hanging on to those challenges allows you to keep that fire burning hot, I say add some more logs to that fire!"

Simon relaxed a bit and smiled. "Thank you, honey. It is important that all my students and staff at the university—as well as my friends, neighbors, and fellow community members—know that our heavenly Father will soon judge all of us. So we need to show we are worthy of Him each and every day. I cannot and will not waver on something as important as eternal salvation!"

"Like I said, keep it burning hot!" Tiffany hugged him and walked toward the kitchen. "Dinner will be ready in half an hour."

"I'll be in my office until then," Simon replied. He shut his office door behind him. He had not let on to his wife that something else was bothering him—a very serious matter. One of his students was accusing him of sexual misconduct. She had sent him an e-mail earlier that day letting him know she was reporting it to the police. She did not think the university would believe her and, even if they did, would not do anything about it.

Dean Clarke had replied to the student's e-mail. He offered to meet with her so he could "clarify his intentions and help her understand the impact of lying to authorities." He was sure the situation would rectify itself if he could just speak with the student, but he was shocked when he saw her next e-mail:

I am afraid of you. The police know what you did, and you will be hearing from them soon.

Clarke slammed his fist on his desk, and his laptop shut. He stood and paced back and forth in his office. He thought about how such an accusation could ruin everything he had worked so hard to accomplish. He quickly decided it was a young student's word against his. He was an upstanding citizen and esteemed professor of religion. Besides, Dean Clarke knew the police chief, mayor, judges, and several other respected community leaders personally. Surely, they would know that these accusations were lies.

He prayed for this storm in his life to pass and joined his wife for dinner. Clarke acted as if nothing were wrong.

The Interrogation

The next morning, while in his campus office, the phone rang. "This is Dean Clarke." He greeted the caller sternly; the call was from an unknown number.

"Hello, Mr. Clarke. This is Officer Ruben Gomez, special liaison to SCU from the police department. I need to speak with you in person. I will be on campus today and would like to stop by to see you at two. Can you please confirm your building and office number?" Officer Gomez seemed cheerful.

"It's Dean Clarke, and today does not work for me," Clarke retorted. "I have existing obligations, so I'm unavailable all day today. What is this visit regarding?"

Officer Gomez was taken aback by the smug response. "I understand you're very busy, so let me know what time you're available tomorrow, and I will stop by then."

Now Dean Clarke was clearly agitated. He asked again, louder, "Why are you coming down here to talk to me? I am very busy and don't have time for unproductive or unnecessary meetings with the local police!"

Officer Gomez did not flinch but asked calmly, "Would it be more convenient for you if we have our conversation at a time that may be in front of your colleagues or students?"

"How dare you threaten me! I suggest you do a little more research on me and talk to your chief before treating me like a common criminal," Clarke yelled into the phone.

Officer Gomez was now getting irritated, so he replied, "I am sorry you feel that way, sir. I simply want to meet with you, and you are not cooperating. If you just give me a time when you are available tomorrow, we can both get off this call and on with our day."

Dean Clarke could see he was not going to shake Officer Gomez easily, so he snapped, "Fine. Be at my office by eight tomorrow morning. I have a busy day, so if you're late, we'll have to find another time next week."

Officer Gomez replied pleasantly, "Thank you, Dean Clarke. We are set for eight o'clock tomorrow, and I look forward—" *Click.* Dean Clarke had hung up on him.

Ruben Gomez knew he had his work cut out for him. He did not know Dean Clarke personally, but almost everyone in the community knew who he was and how connected he was with the local political and business leaders.

The next morning, Officer Gomez arrived on campus in street clothes and an unmarked car to avoid drawing attention to the meeting. After he had entered the building, he asked a couple of students where Dean Clarke's office was, and they pointed him in the right direction.

Officer Gomez arrived ten minutes early and was greeted by a cheerful woman at the front desk. The plaque on her desk read *Assistant to the Dean.*

"Good morning, Officer Gomez. Dean Clarke will not be available until eight. Please take a seat, and I will call you when he is ready."

Ruben took a seat, and at precisely eight o'clock, the cheerful assistant said, "Dean Clarke will see you now."

Ruben thanked the assistant and entered the office marked *Dean of Religious Studies* on its door. Dean Clarke was sitting at his desk, writing. He did not look up when he said, "Welcome. Please have a seat, and I will be with you in a moment."

After a minute of silence, Dean Clarke put the pen down, looked up, and said, "How can I help you?"

Gomez replied, "Thank you for meeting with me today. As you are probably aware, one of your students has filed a complaint against you. I am here to get your statement. Can you tell me how you know this student?"

Dean Clarke stared at Officer Gomez for a few seconds before he said, "Did you do any research on me like I suggested?"

"No, I did not do any research on you beyond what the student has told me," Ruben replied.

"Well, I have done some research on you," Clarke said smugly, "and you have quite the track record."

Officer Gomez did not say a word, but he already assumed what he must have found with a simple search on the Internet. He figured he might even know more if he had friends down at the department.

Dean Clarke continued, "It seems as if you like to beat up innocent victims and also to jump behind the wheel of a car with a blood-alcohol level twice the legal limit." Dean Clarke stood up, smiling. It was like a game of chess in which Clarke was gleefully declaring, "Check!"

Gomez shifted a bit in his seat and said, "Sir, I am not here to discuss my past sins. I am here to get a statement from you on what happened with this student."

"Funny you should use that word," Dean Clarke said, "because I have dedicated my life to helping others stamp out sin to live a life that delivers eternal salvation. Do you attend church regularly? Do you pray every day? Do you help the sick and the poor? Do you tithe? Do you even know what any of that means? Because I do, and I live it each and every day. What about you?"

Officer Gomez stood up, grabbed his notebook, and said, "Obviously, this is not a good time for you. I will come back another time when you might be more open to discussing your activities with the student. You will hear from me again later this week."

As Officer Gomez headed to the door, Dean Clarke said, "You got off with a slap on the wrist. You didn't even serve the punishment required for repentance, and now you are down here questioning me. No, you are down here judging me, after all I do for this community. You might want to think twice before coming here again." Dean Clarke stood behind his desk, the tips of his fingers touching the desktop.

Nobody had ever spoken to Officer Gomez this way, so with the shock quickly wearing off, he offered one final response. "A student has allegedly been hurt, and it is my job to find out what really happened. I owe it to her to get to the truth, and the more you try to slither out of my questions, the more emboldened I am to get them from you. You might want to think of the pain this student is in the next time you're patting yourself on the back for another 'good deed' you've done for the community. Have a good day."

Officer Gomez shut the door behind him and left campus.

As he was driving back to the station, Ruben realized he had been seriously unprepared for Dean Clarke. He thought about his past and how hard it had been to forgive himself. If their recent meeting was a heavyweight boxing match, Clarke had landed a right hook that knocked Gomez to the mat. However, Ruben was not about to let himself get knocked out and needed to get up quickly and go another round. He called his wife to let her know he would be home early for dinner. He needed to do some research and learn more about his opponent.

After dinner, Ruben opened up his laptop on the kitchen table. An online search turned up one glowing article after the next on the positive impact Dean Clarke had made at the university and within the community.

However, he found some messages on a social media site that caught his attention. Based on several messages, Ruben was able to gather that Dean Clarke was single into his mid-thirties and that his wife was a former student. Although they did not get married until two years after she graduated, the rumor among the students was that they were dating while she was still a student—a major no-no at SCU. Tiffany, twelve years younger than her husband, had been married to him for four years now.

Officer Gomez knew this history might indicate a pattern of Clarke's dating students. Ruben shut down the computer and went to the bedroom where his wife, Isabella, was reading a book.

He sat next to her on the bed and said, "I have something I need to tell you."

Isabella put down her book and sat up in bed, "What is it, Ruben?"

"My old case might get brought up again, and it could get very public this time. I'm investigating someone who has ties to a lot of people in power, and he's already made it clear that he knows about my past. This person is very offended that I am even questioning him. I have a feeling he'll stop at nothing to deter me from investigating further. I just want you to know in advance that it might be an issue."

Isabella was stunned. "I thought we left all of that behind when we moved here. You have done so well with the rehab and the therapy. I think it has helped with the guilt. You've become a much better father to our kids. Can someone else get assigned to this case?"

"I don't think so, and I don't want to ask. This guy is trying to bully me, and I'm not going to be intimidated even if I have to relive my past," Ruben said, staring at the wall as if his past were flashing on a screen placed there.

The Big Mistake

Officer Gomez had made some serious mistakes. He was making strides in forgiving himself and steering his life in a positive direction. His father and grandfather also had been police officers, so being an officer was all he had ever known or wanted. Ruben had also picked up some less-than-desirable traits from his father, who'd had a drinking and anger problem. At one time, Ruben had picked up right where his father had left off.

It was not uncommon for Ruben to see his father in a fistfight or passed out drunk on the family-room couch. Ruben was actually happy when his father was passed out because that meant neither he nor his two brothers would be on the receiving end of that day's wrath. In his childhood, Ruben saw his father repeat these behaviors. He thought it was normal for a father and police officer to act that way. As a father to a young son and daughter of his own, Ruben Gomez vowed he would be different.

After four years on a police force in his hometown, Ruben ran out of luck when it came to hiding his anger and drinking. He had argued for several months with another police officer on the force, and on one night, they ended up at the same drinking establishment. Ruben had too much to drink as he often did, and the other officer spouted off about the long history of police officers in their town named "Gomez" and their love of drinking. The officer mumbled, "Instead of 'Gomez,' they should just give them badges that say 'Officer Drunk-ez.'"

Ruben snapped, hitting the other officer over the head with a bottle and then punching him repeatedly. The bar brawl was quickly broken up, but Ruben had already shattered the other officer's jaw. He split his head open so badly that it required sixteen stitches. In a drunken panic, Ruben ran to his car and sped away. After only a few blocks, Ruben was in a minor auto accident near the center of town. The police arrived within minutes, and Ruben Gomez was placed in the back of a patrol car immediately. Not long after those incidents, the local media arrived. Ruben's secret was out, and now it was front-page news in his hometown paper.

Ruben and his family endured a long and embarrassing trial, but the outcome was as good as they could have hoped. His attorney orchestrated a brilliant defense. He convinced the judge that it was all due to a hereditary alcohol dependency and job-related stress as a third-generation police officer. Ruben pleaded no contest to lesser charges and two years' probation. The plea deal also required Ruben to resign from the police force. He had to attend an inpatient anger-management and alcohol-rehabilitation program. Ruben's attorney told him this was the only way to have any chance of working as a police officer again.

Two days after the trial, Ruben went away to the treatment center and learned his problems were even deeper than he had realized. All of those years witnessing his father mentally and physically abuse his mother and brothers had created deep-rooted issues of anger and bitterness. Ruben was unhappy with who he had become and blamed his father. Despite all the therapy and counselors, Ruben did not forgive his father and left the treatment center sober but still angry.

Fortunately, Ruben's wife, Isabella, had a steady job at the local hospital and stood by him during the trial, even after all the years of drinking and fighting. The court of public opinion was not as kind to Ruben. Many felt he received preferential treatment because he was a third-generation police officer. His reputation was so poor in his hometown that he was unable to secure any type of employment. All Ruben ever knew or wanted was to be a police officer and that was not possible in his hometown. So after successfully completing his two years of probation, Ruben convinced Isabella that they should move so he could reestablish his career as a police officer. Opportunity after opportunity was thwarted after each department conducted a background check on Ruben. After several months, the police department's hiring manager in the small town that hosted SCU said he believed Ruben deserved a second chance. It was the only community that extended an employment offer to Ruben to be a police officer.

Ruben and Isabella were excited about having a new start. Isabella quickly got a new job at a health center, and their two children adapted quickly to kindergarten and first grade. Isabella also wanted Ruben and herself to find a local church to attend. She had visited a couple of churches in the area and found one she loved. The pastor delivered passionate sermons of grace, love, and peace.

In the past, Ruben had been resistant to attending church. He had said, "If I go inside a church, don't stand next to me since I will probably get struck down for all I have done." However, Isabella was worried about Ruben's guilt issues and potential latent anger. She thought the move would be a great opportunity to approach Ruben about going to church with her.

"Ruben, I found a great church and would like you and the kids to start going with me," Isabella said one evening after turning off the television.

"I told you about church and me. I'm glad you found one you like. You know I believe in God, but I just don't want to be part of a church right now." Ruben stared at the blacked-out television screen.

"This one is different," said Isabella, scooting closer to Ruben on the couch. "Everyone is so friendly and loving. Their children's ministry is outstanding. Plus, they accept everyone for who they are. I think you would like it."

"I thought you said you were going to church. That doesn't sound like any church I've ever been to," Ruben said. He tried to mask his defensiveness with humor.

"I'm serious, Ruben. I think it would be really good for you. Forgiving others helped you during your alcohol rehab," Isabella said, raising her voice in frustration.

"That was different. I don't want to get judged for my past anymore. Been there, done that. I'm not going to do it again," Ruben yelled back at Isabella.

Isabella felt hurt but determined, "I can't believe you won't do something that is actually good for you and very important to me. I have stood by you through the drinking, the fights—our fights—the trial, and now, the move. I practically raised the kids as a single mom for many years. I don't ask you for much, but this is very important to me, and I don't—"

"OK, OK...I'll go!" Ruben yelled, standing up.

Isabella, walking to the bedroom, said, "Good. We'll go to the ten-thirty service on Sunday." She closed the door behind her.

Ruben began attending church regularly with his family every Sunday.

A few days had passed since his confrontation with Clarke, and Ruben decided to swing by the campus unannounced to see if he could catch the dean in his office. Gomez walked right past the dean's assistant and into Dean Clarke's office. Clarke was sitting at his desk, writing again. This time, he looked up right away, agitated, and said, "Can I help you?"

"It looks like this is a good time for you, so I am going to ask you a few questions," Ruben said, taking a seat. Catching Dean Clarke off guard, Gomez launched his line of questioning. He asked about the female student who was making the accusations, and Dean Clarke responded with short, smug answers. Gomez realized he was not getting much valid information, so he asked abruptly, "How did you meet your wife?"

"Excuse me?"

"Pretty simple question. How did you meet your wife, Tiffany?" *Check Mate*, Ruben thought to himself.

"Oh, I see you have finally done some research on me. Surprised it took so long but, nonetheless, my relationship with Tiffany was completely platonic while she was a student here. Not until after she graduated did it progress to something intimate. Anyone who says anything to the contrary is simply spreading tales," Dean Clarke stated proudly.

"So the rumors that you have a weakness for the attractive female students are completely baseless?" Ruben rebutted, irritated with the professor's games.

Dean Clarke stood up quickly, leaned across the desk, and said, "Watch yourself, Officer Gomez. I have been very understanding and helpful in this matter up to this point, but again, you seem to be looking for someone to crucify, and I will not allow it to continue. All I see is an angry drunk who is now sober but still angry. I am sorry that your lifestyle and sins have led you to the situation you are in today, but you should seriously consider taking the necessary steps to repent while you still can. Instead of tearing others down to build yourself up, focus on the good you should be doing to please God. Stop chasing down an innocent man who's spent his entire life trying to save people and guide them toward eternal life in Heaven. Go find some real criminals so you can prove your worth in this world. Don't be a bad cop; be a good police officer. Am I clear?"

Ruben felt as if Dean Clarke had landed a sucker punch right in his gut. He did not know how to respond to this tirade, so he stood up and said, "Thank you for your time, Dean. Your answers have been extremely helpful. I will be in touch soon if I have more questions for you."

"So happy I could be of assistance," Dean Clarke said, dripping with sarcasm.

A Better Cop

A few weeks later, the chief of police approached Gomez after roll call one morning. The chief told Ruben he was being assigned to a security detail for the mayor's Annual Prayer Dinner. The mayor and several other political, business, and church leaders would be in attendance, so a robust security detail would be needed.

Gomez was excited to be part of the security detail for one of the biggest events in town. The case with Dean Clarke was going nowhere, so the change of scenery would be welcomed.

Ruben went home, pressed his uniform, and polished his medals and shoes to look his best. On the day of the event, he arrived a couple hours early to familiarize himself with the facility and meet with the head of the security detail. Ruben picked up an event program to learn which guests would be in attendance. After getting halfway down the list, his heart sank. He had hoped to forget about Dean Clarke, who would be the event's keynote speaker. A range of emotions shot through Ruben. He was angry, anxious, and even a little afraid. Gomez knew the dean had a way with words that could not be matched. He did not want to get into a verbal spar with him in public—not with what Dean Clarke knew about him.

Gomez went to the restroom to splash cold water onto his face and then called Isabella for some emotional support. "How's my lovely wife doing tonight?"

"Pretty good. How's the mayor's dinner?"

"OK, I guess. You'll never believe who the main speaker is tonight—the guy I told you about who's giving me all those problems during my investigation. He makes me nervous." Ruben shuffled his feet as he talked.

"Why would you be nervous?" Isabella asked innocently.

"Because...the way he talks. He has a way of making me feel so guilty and ashamed. I told you he knew about my past. I wouldn't be one bit surprised if he decides to shame me publicly. He just makes me feel like I am a bad person, a bad cop and that I am not good enough." Ruben's voice started to waver and crack.

"You have nothing to worry about, honey," Isabella said cheerfully. "God has already forgiven you for all your sins. You have no reason to feel ashamed because Jesus gave his life. And no one can make you feel a certain way. If you're feeling ashamed, that's coming from you—let it go, baby."

"You're right," Ruben said sullenly. "It's just hard to remind myself of that when someone is on the attack. I have to go. I'll talk to you later." Ruben hung up and took his post inside the door to the main floor as he watched the first guests arrive.

About midway through the event, Ruben found himself enjoying the mayor's Prayer Dinner. Business, political, and religious leaders took turns at the podium. They told stories of heroism, charity, and helping neighbors and ended with short prayers for the community. The mood was positive, and all of them seemed to be enjoying themselves.

Ruben was especially excited to see Pastor Scott onstage; he was head of the church that he and Isabella attended. The pastor told a story about two local brothers who stopped talking to each other after a big argument.

Days turned to weeks, weeks became years, and soon, a full decade passed without either brother exchanging a word. One brother got married and started attending Pastor Scott's church with his wife. One Sunday, Pastor Scott was talking about the parable of the prodigal son and how the heavenly Father forgave everyone. The older brother was so moved by the story that he reached out to his younger brother immediately. Over time, they reconciled and are getting closer every day. Pastor Scott said that those brothers were our community's version of the prodigal son and that everyone in the room is blessed by the grace of God the Father. Ruben wanted nothing more than to feel that grace.

Pastor Scott left the podium, and the moment Officer Gomez had dreaded was about to occur. Dean Clarke took the stage amid applause, immediately reciting a long list of personal and community accomplishments for which he was responsible. Gomez had to admit that the list was impressive, but he was sure the professor would wake up with a sore shoulder after giving himself so many pats on the back.

Clarke talked about his vision and hope for the community. Then, he transitioned into speaking about accountability and being a role model for righteousness, pure living, and general obedience to God. Gomez noticed some people fidgeted uncomfortably in their seats as Dean Clarke got louder and more animated in his speech about repentance and judgment.

"It is my hope that people who are hiding behind jealousy, bitterness, and especially anger get the help they need now before it is too late—before standing in judgment before God!" Dean Clarke proclaimed to the audience.

Gomez was pretty sure these were jabs directed at him, noticing that Dean Clarke stared in his direction during the comments.

Clarke continued, "If anyone in this room wants to know which path is the right one, look at me as a living example of how one should live. If you are still unsure, please come see me so I can help you overcome your bitterness and anger."

Now, Gomez *knew* Dean Clarke was speaking to him directly, and he felt warm adrenaline creeping up his body. At first, he felt intense anger as he always had in the past. Then suddenly, he thought of what Pastor Scott had preached about forgiveness. Now it was clearer than ever before. At that moment, Ruben finally realized he no longer needed to live in shame or regret. He was forgiven for his mistakes. Ruben smiled, filled with joy. An elephant-sized weight was lifted off his shoulders.

He almost forgot Dean Clarke was still speaking until he heard, "I hope everyone has learned a valuable lesson tonight and that we can all benefit from my words. I am sure everyone would like to go home now to be with their families. So unless someone else would like to offer any words, I will close this dinner with a final prayer."

"Wait!" came a yell from the back of the room.

Ruben noticed that everyone was looking at him. He realized he had let his emotions get the best of him. He was the one who had yelled out.

"Oh, Officer Gomez, do you have something to add?" Dean Clarke asked from the podium.

Ruben walked to the stage toward Dean Clarke. The room seemed quiet, and he felt warm with all eyes focused in his direction.

When Ruben got to the bottom of the stage, Clarke looked down at him and said, "I hoped someone would take my words to heart. Would you like to repent in front of this audience so you can share your regret with God for your actions and hope for forgiveness?"

Ruben climbed the stairs to the stage and took the microphone. He walked a few feet to his right and looked out over the audience. He shook inside with anxiety but became so overcome with peace that he almost felt the words coming out before he was ready. "Dean Clarke, thank you for all you have done for this community. You know more about religion and the Bible than I probably ever will in my entire life.

"I know, but thank you, Officer Gomez."

"However," Officer Gomez continued, "there is one thing you are absolutely wrong about. I do not need to hope for forgiveness because I have already been forgiven. That happened the day Jesus died on the cross for all of us and all of our sins!"

"Bravo!" said Dean Clarke, clapping. "That was quite the performance. However, I thought you would have used this forum to ask for forgiveness for your past, but if you are not ready, then we should just proceed with the final prayer."

"I am sorry for everything I have done in my past, but I have changed, and I am forgiven. I am so thankful to my family, the police chief, my pastor, and the whole community for giving me a second chance. I am humbled by your grace, and in return, I will serve this community to the best of my ability." A smattering of applause came from the audience.

This angered Dean Clarke even more, so he yelled out, "You still have anger problems. I have seen it myself. You have not changed, and you have not followed the necessary steps to be forgiven! True forgiveness requires action, and you should be ashamed of yourself standing up here and—"

"Please stop," came from behind both Dean Clarke and Officer Gomez on the stage. It was Pastor Scott who could not stand to hear Dean Clarke belittling Officer Gomez. Pastor Scott knew about Ruben's past and was proud of how he had turned his life around.

"Pastor Scott, you sat in my classes several years ago," the professor replied. "You have no authority to ask me to stop, so I will continue—"

"But *I* do!" It was the mayor, looking frustrated as a few gasps came from the audience. The mayor said again, "I do, Dean Clarke. This is my event, and your address is over. I will close in prayer."

The mayor said a quick prayer and wished everyone a good evening. Few people left their seats because they wanted to see what drama would unfold between Professor Simon Clarke and Officer Ruben Gomez.

Ruben realized he was still on security detail and returned as fast as he could to his post near the rear doors. As he walked back, a couple of claps led to more clapping. Eventually, he received a standing ovation from the crowd. He was so shocked that he did not know what to do, so he waved and stood at attention by the exit doors.

As everyone was leaving, many people addressed Ruben to tell him how much they admired his courage. Several said he was a good cop, and Ruben had never felt so proud in his entire life.

When Ruben got home, he told Isabella, and she could not believe it. "So you were listening all those mornings I thought you were dozing off in church." The couple laughed for the first time in ages.

Two days later, Gomez was back on duty and went to the station to clock in for his shift. He noticed Dean Clarke and his lawyer were meeting with a detective. Officer Gomez stopped in his tracks. "Did you hear the news?" the police chief asked him.

"No, what happened?"

"Another female student came forward yesterday. She said she was inspired by some cop's speech at the mayor's event. She has texts and e-mails proving that Dean Clarke crossed the line with her, too. Detectives are looking into charges and will take it from here."

Ruben Gomez sat in a quiet corner in the back of the officer's locker room and prayed. Afterward, he walked back out to the dispatch board, and feeling as confident as ever; he asked the chief, "What do you have next for me? I am ready for anything!"

Overview

This story is the modern refresh of the parable of the Pharisee and tax collector in Luke 18:9–14. In this modern remake of the story, Professor Simon Clarke is the self-righteous and overzealously religious Pharisee, and Officer Ruben Gomez is the despised sinner and tax collector. In both stories, the sinner was humble and forgiven. This story is a great reminder of how poisonous pride can be—even pride in one's religious knowledge—and that humility is chief of all Christian virtues.

Moral of the Story: It's not how visibly or loudly you praise God or even follow the "rules." It is about trusting in God and submitting to His will so your actions—not just your words—reflect your love and praise.

DEBT FORGIVENESS

Kevin poked Joe in the ribs with his pen so he would look up from his book. "Joe—you've got to check this out."

"Ouch! Check out what?" Joe jumped and replied loudly. That prompted other students at the long table to look over at them. They were in seventh-period library, and talking loud was strictly prohibited. It also attracted a lot of attention.

Kevin ducked down in his seat as if his six-foot-two frame would be harder to see. He whispered, "Short-stack Zack is going to make his move on Stephanie. This is going to be epic!"

Kevin was the starting left fielder, and Joe was the star first baseman for the Liberty High School varsity baseball team. The Liberty High School baseball team won the state championship two out of the last five years, and most of the players were well-known throughout the school and the community. Many of the students paid attention to what the players were doing, so when some of the students saw Kevin and Joe laughing and looking across the library at the table with Zack and Stephanie, they joined in watching.

Zack was also on the baseball team, but as the back-up second baseman, he rarely saw much action on the diamond. He was the shortest guy on the team, and his teammates reminded him of his lack of stature with the nickname Short-stack Zack. Despite Zack's frequent protests that he did not like the nickname, that seemed all the more reason for his teammates to ensure that the nickname stuck.

Earlier that week, Zack was talking to Kevin in the dugout in the late innings of a blowout game. He told Kevin he was interested in Stephanie on the dance team. Zack thought she was interested in him, too, because she had asked him to help with her Advanced Algebra homework. Zack helped Stephanie with her homework during the seventh period in the library over the past three weeks, and he told Kevin he was going to ask Stephanie out this Friday.

Amused, Kevin told Zack he agreed that Stephanie was definitely into him and highly encouraged Zack to ask her out. Stephanie was one of the prettiest sopho-more girls in the school, and Kevin was sure Zack would get served a big piece of humble pie. Kevin liked Zack but enjoyed picking on him for his height even more. The same was true for most of the other players. Most of them liked Zack, but he always got angry when they would make fun of his size; for high-school boys, that was too much gold not to mine on a regular basis.

Kevin and Joe were joined by the other students at their table as they watched Zack build up the nerve to ask Stephanie out. The bell was about to ring in a couple of minutes, and they knew he would have to act soon.

Suddenly, they saw Zack push away the math book as Stephanie stood up quickly; she grabbed it before it flew off the table. As she was putting the book back into her backpack and walk away, she shouted, "I thought you were trying to help me as a friend. Don't ever text me again!"

Seconds later, Stephanie was out the door. Joe stood up and started clapping. Kevin and another student joined in quickly. The librarian, who was also the girls' volleyball coach, stood up and said, "All of you—stop that immediately. I am going to—"

The bell rang, and the students jumped up and began scurrying for the door. Seemingly exhausted and not interested in a protracted fight, the librarian said to the offenders as they walked out, "Don't let that happen in my library again!"

Zack sat at the table in disbelief. He wondered how he could have read Stephanie so wrong and how his teammates seemed to relish his demise. His desire to prove all of them wrong was growing stronger with each day.

The library incident was a common occurrence in Zack's tenure at Liberty High School. He was frequently the butt of jokes and constantly teased about his height. Zack would get frustrated because most of the boys in his class felt superior to him just because they were taller. They did not care if he was a good athlete and one of the smartest students; they judged him simply based on the numbers from a measuring tape. He was Short-stack Zack and nothing more to most of them.

Zack was always considered smart. He excelled in math, finance, and accounting, especially. Zack's problems in high school were never related to academics, but his social life was another story.

Zack was only five foot five entering his senior year, and he had not grown since he was in eighth grade. His father was five feet seven, and his mother was right at five feet, so Zack knew this was as good as it was going to get, height wise. Most of his female classmates considered Zack average to good looking. He had an athletic build and was well groomed; he wore stylish clothes and had short chestnut-brown hair. Despite those traits, his height combined with glasses and teenage acne had Zack going solo to most school dances and events.

Zack used the ridicule as fuel to excel in school so that someday, he could be more successful than anyone else in his class. He often dreamed of attending his ten-year class reunion to brag about his success.

Once Zack entered his senior year, he withdrew from sports and most of his former so-called friends. Instead, he focused on academics so he could go to a good college as far away as possible. The only friend he maintained was his neighbor, Todd, because he never teased Zack about his height.

Todd lived a few streets away from Zack, and they had been casual friends since grade school. Todd was a little overweight. Much like Zack and his height, everyone seemed to focus on Todd and his weight. Todd was witty, funny, and so talented on several band instruments that he was receiving scholarship offers from multiple colleges in his junior year. Zack used to get frustrated with Todd because he had no interest in sports and would rather play video games or go camping. However, now Zack appreciated Todd because he did not judge anybody else.

Todd and Zack became closer as they progressed through their senior year. One day, while sitting in the game room at Zack's house, he asked Todd what he planned to do after high school.

"I don't know yet. I've narrowed down the scholarship offers to three schools, and only one of them is in the state. It's at the Christian university that both my parents went to so that one is probably the front-runner. What about you?"

"Getting out of here as fast as I can," Zack said with a smile.

"Where are you going?"

"I'm going to that private university in the northeast. I got a partial academic scholarship, so that will be a big help. They have one of the best finance and accounting dual-degree programs in the country, so that's what I'm going to do."

"Wow! That's awesome, Zack. Congratulations."

"Don't congratulate me yet. I won't rest until I can come back here and show everyone how successful I am, especially those losers on the baseball team who all think they're better than everyone else."

Todd stated, "I heard some scouts think Joe is good enough to get drafted by a major league baseball team. If he does, that may be tough to top at the class reunion."

"I'm not worried about Joe or any of those other guys becoming more successful than me. I can't wait until that reunion, and I haven't even graduated yet."

The room was quiet for a moment when Zack broke the silence and said, "Speaking of graduating, I need to get studying so I can ace this test and get out of here. I'll catch up with you at school tomorrow." Todd left, and Zack began studying for his finance test.

Soon, their senior year came to a close; both Todd and Zack graduated. Todd moved less than an hour away to his parents' alma mater while Zack moved over fifteen hundred miles away to his new college campus.

Financial Future

College was much kinder to Zack than high school. Professors appreciated Zack for his knowledge, tenacity, and work ethic; he was rewarded with accolades and high grades. Zack excelled in all of his finance, economics, business, and accounting classes. As a result, he befriended many of his classmates who shared similar interests.

Zack was happy heading into his senior year because he was finally getting the respect he long deserved. He was less bitter, and with his improving attitude, Zack even managed to have a couple of girlfriends during his first three years in college. However, all of that changed the day Zack heard that his old high-school nemesis, Joe, was drafted in the third round of the Major League Baseball First-Year Player Draft. Not only did Joe get a full scholarship to a prestigious university, but he was also on the fast track to becoming the financial success and household name that Zack intended for himself exclusively. Zack knew something had to change.

Similar to his senior year in high school, Zack made becoming wildly successful his number-one priority. He rarely went out with old friends and even took a part-time job at a small local bank to gain more knowledge on the banking and finance industry. He had little time for anything else that did not complement his quest to be the best in his class.

Zack was brilliant in finance, but he was also ruthless in his quest for personal success. It wasn't long before he noticed how the small bank where he worked was missing out on major profit opportunities. It did not collect fees on transactions that other banks charged their customers routinely. Zack saw this as an opportunity to showcase his brilliance, so he developed a recommended menu of fees, justification within the local market, and the resulting profit potential if his recommendations were enacted. Zack set up a meeting and presented his recommendations to the bank president directly. The president loved the profit potential, so he approved the fees and even put Zack in charge of implementation. Immediately, Zack took charge of new fee execution.

As Zack neared the end of his senior year in college, he began to look for his first full-time job after graduation. He was one of the top students within the College of Finance and Accounting, so he had multiple offers in different states. However, Zack wanted to either go back to his hometown or continue to work at his current bank, where he was developing a good relationship with the owner and president. He felt his best opportunity to get on the fast track to success was with his current employer at the local bank, so Zack committed to pursuing that option right after finals and graduation.

Zack took three weeks off from work to focus on finals. On the day he returned back to work, he was excited to tell the bank president that he was willing to become a full-time manager now that he had graduated. Zack was sure the president would be excited that he had chosen them over all of his other exciting options. However, Zack was surprised to meet resistance to his generous offer upon his return to work.

The bank president called Zack into his office and said that they were achieving record profits, but many long-term customers were complaining about the fees. He told Zack, "We have many long- and short-term customers who are unhappy with the dramatic addition and escalation of fees; some are even leaving us. I think we added too much, too fast."

Zack paused in shock and then rebutted, "I believe you just said profits were at record highs. Isn't that what every business wants? Isn't that what you want?"

"Not this way. We are going to have to cut back on some of the fees."

Zack was floored. He thought, *How could any company make record profits and be disappointed?* Flippantly, Zack responded, "Then I guess I wouldn't be a very good fit here. I work hard to make money for myself and my employer. I'm not afraid to listen to a few complaints or ruffle a few feathers to get there."

"You're probably right, Zack. I thank you for all you have given us, and I wish you well in the future, wherever that may be," the bank president stated. "If you'll excuse me, I have another meeting to attend."

Zack was dumbfounded at the stupidity of the bank president. He could not understand his decision. Zack had no choice now but to go back home. He continued to think about his next move during his two-day drive back to his parents' house in his hometown.

Despite the sheer horror that he failed to execute his master plan of securing a good job right after graduation, Zack was not completely disappointed because he would be back home with his parents, William, and Kristen. They had always been fair with Zack and supportive of him. His father, William, owned a small but thriving business with a team of four tax attorneys. He was pretty tough on Zack and his younger brother, Josh, when they were growing up. He would tell Zack and Josh that he was trying to instill in them the work ethic and tenacity that were needed to succeed in business—and life.

"Hi, honey. Welcome home," Zack's mom, Kristen, said as she met Zack walking up the driveway.

"Hi, Mom. Great to be back, but hopefully, it won't be too long," Zack replied while giving his mom a hug.

"You are welcome to stay as long as you need."

"Thanks. Where's Dad?"

"He's still at the office. He mentioned they're pitching a new corporate client next week and that he may be late tonight. You know your father won't come home until it's perfect."

"That's for sure. I'm going to get unpacked now."

Zack began unpacking in his old room. He noticed old pictures of high-school graduation, prom, and summer vacations; he smiled. His smile quickly faded when he noticed the picture of the baseball team. He thought Kevin looked even more clueless than Zack remembered, and Joe had that same "I am so perfect" smile that was burned into Zack's memory. He began to daydream about the look on Joe's face when they saw each other at the ten-year class reunion, and Joe realized that Zack was the more successful one between them. Zack said to himself aloud, "I've gotta get a job fast, or I'm going to fall behind. Time to get moving."

A week after Zack arrived back home, he was reviewing jobs on his laptop when his mom came in with some good news. "Guess who's coming back home this summer?"

"Who?"

"Todd just graduated from Intermountain Christian University and is coming home for the summer. I spoke with his mom, and she says he's going to seminary in the fall."

"Wow! That's big news. I haven't spoken with Todd in over six months, so I'll reach out to him after he gets home."

Zack's mom looked over his shoulder at his computer screen and asked, "Any luck?"

"Nothing I would consider. I did hear that First National Bank here in town is looking for a new assistant branch manager, but I am waaaayyyyyy too overqualified for that position." Zack replied with a look on his face as if he just ate raw liver.

"Well, I hope you find whatever you're looking for," Kristen said as she left the room.

Later that evening, Zack and his brother, Josh, were watching TV when their father came home. He put down his briefcase and immediately went into his home office. A few minutes later, he came to his door and said in his usual commanding voice, "Zack, please come to my office. I need to speak with you."

Zack was still a little intimidated by his father, even as a twenty-two-year-old college graduate. He walked quickly down the hall and sat in the chair across from William's desk. "Hey Dad. What's up?"

"Did you hear about the opening at First National Bank?"

"I did, but I'm still looking for something better suited for my skill set," Zack said, starting to get a little defensive. He had heard that tone from his father before.

"Are you looking to start off as the president or CEO of a company, or are you willing to work hard and prove yourself so you can move up quickly?" William retorted.

"Of course, nothing less than CEO would be worth my time and effort," Zack said sarcastically and continued. "You know I'm willing to work hard. I always have, and I always will, but I would like it to be just a little higher up the ladder, so I don't have as far to climb to the top."

"Son, I know you are willing to work hard. I never question your drive or work ethic, but I think that you may be underestimating the opportunity at First National. That is all I am saying," William stated in his calm courtroom voice.

"What do you mean by *underestimating*?" Zack responded with curiosity.

"First, the job is open right now, right here where you are living today. Second, the president's sons and daughters have all moved away. There is no succession plan, and retirement is not too far away for the president. Third, I don't think they have been the best-run bank, in my opinion, and someone smart—like you—could really stand out."

William paused for a second and looked Zack right in the eye. "You can also reach the top rung on the ladder pretty fast if you climb two at a time!"

Zack was warming up to the idea. He could start making money right away while gaining some valuable experience to help him climb the ladder. Zack was willing to put forth the effort to advance as fast as possible, so he decided to send his resume.

Succeed or Bust

After two interviews, Zack was offered the position of assistant branch manager. Just five weeks into the job, he noticed some of the same opportunities to grow profits as he did while working at the local bank back in college. However, this time, Zack wanted the fees to stick, so he devised a plan to implement new fees in a more covert manner.

His plan was to charge new customers the fees, but not existing customers. Then, he would create a new menu of checking and savings account options with exciting but cost-effective perks that also came with new fees. He was certain that over time, most customers would choose voluntarily to add the fees Zack needed to maximize profits.

It worked.

Twenty months after he started, over 60 percent of the accounts at First National Bank had new fees applied. The bank was doing so well financially that the president, Mr. Grabowski, told Zack that he planned to open a new branch on the west side of the city. He wanted Zack to become the branch manager at the new location.

Zack was excited to hear the good news. He would be the youngest branch manager of any bank in the city and still on the fast track to being hugely successful.

A little over a year later, after Zack had been branch manager at the new location for ten months, he received a call from Mr. Grabowski one morning. He told Zack he had received the latest quarterly financials and wanted to meet Zack for a business lunch at the local country club to review them together.

Zack was anxious to hear what Mr. Grabowski wanted to discuss in the meeting. Business at Zack's branch was doing very well, but Mr. Grabowski had never invited him to lunch before. So Zack was not sure what to expect when he sat down at the table for lunch.

"Good afternoon, Zack. Thank you for meeting me on such short notice."

"No problem, Mr. Grabowski. I'm happy to meet with you anytime."

"Excellent. By the way, you can call me Charlie."

"Well, thank you Mr. Grabows...I mean, Charlie!" Zack replied nervously, and they both laughed.

"Zack, I won't beat around the bush any longer. The numbers at your branch are exceeding all expectations. New customer accounts are up, revenue is up, and most importantly, your branch is already more profitable than I ever would have projected nearly one year after opening a new branch. That is quite an accomplishment. You have a natural instinct for banking."

"Thank you, Mr. Grabowski. I work very hard, and it's very rewarding to hear you say that."

"Please Zack, call me Charlie."

"Oh. OK, sir," Zack replied, feeling uncomfortable about the growing causal relationship with the bank president. That went against everything he was taught by his parents.

"Zack, but that is not the real reason I asked you to lunch today," Charlie Grabowski said, as he took a sip of water.

"You know that all of my children have decided to build their careers outside of banking. I started this bank myself with some money my father left me nearly forty years ago, and I couldn't be prouder of where it is today. My original intent was to make this a family business that I could pass on to my kids and then eventually to my grandchildren. Unfortunately, that is not going to happen, so now I am going to Plan B. Plan B is to find a partner who can make this bank even more successful so that I know First National Bank will be around for a very long time, even after I am no longer around."

Mr. Grabowski paused again. Both he and Zack took sips of their water.

"Zack, that is where you come into the picture. My wife, Gina, and I have been discussing the right time for me to retire, and that time is getting closer. Therefore, I would like to make you my first partner in the business and pass the torch to you as the future bank president." Charlie concluded with a smile.

Zack was overwhelmed with happiness. He could not stop smiling even when he responded, "Mr., or, I mean, Charlie—I can't thank you enough for this opportunity. I am very honored you would consider me, and I won't let you down."

"Zack, I know you are still young, and this is very early in your career, but you have the intellect and the drive to succeed that I haven't seen since I was your age. I believe your natural instincts and young exuberance combined with my knowledge and experience will make us a good team. Plus, this won't come without a lot of hard work over the next eighteen months. I need you to continue to run the branch but also shadow me as much as possible. That way, you'll know how to be the bank president when I retire in a little over a year. I couldn't think of anyone else who would put forth the effort to succeed like you do."

Charlie and Zack continued to discuss the opportunity during lunch. Zack was ecstatic about the partner opportunity and could not wait to go home and tell his parents.

Zack was still living at home, so when he arrived later that evening during dinner, he sat down and said, "Guess what? I have some good news and some bad news to share with both of you."

His parents looked at each other with concerned looks, and his mom said, "OK. What is it?"

"The bad news is that I am moving out into my own apartment as soon as possible."

"I thought you said you had some bad news, Zack!" his mom replied while giving her husband a knuckle bump.

"Ha-ha. Funny, Mom. Just don't cry when I leave this time," Zack said sarcastically.

"The good news is that I am going to be a partner and bank president in a little over a year. A bank president can't be living at home with his parents!"

His mother stood up and hugged Zack. "Honey that is great news. We're so proud of you."

Zack looked over to his father, who said, "Zack, I told you that was the right move a few years ago. You have put in the effort, and now you are reaping what you have sown. Great job!"

That was high praise coming from Zack's father. The three of them continued to discuss the new partnership and Zack's bright future.

Welcome Mr. President

Four months after becoming the full-time bank president, Zack celebrated his twenty-sixth birthday. He calculated his new net worth as the co-owner of First National Bank, and it was just over a million dollars. Zack smiled when he thought of his ten-year high school reunion in two years. Everything was starting to line up as he planned. Now he needed to grow his net worth even more.

It did not take long for Zack to put his mark on First National Bank. He noticed that many of the auto loans First National Bank provided were past due. First National Bank was one of the largest local lenders for cars, trucks, boats, and even small businesses. Zack calculated the additional profit the bank could make if he cut the past-due loans in half, and it was a big number. As a small, community-based bank, First National Bank had a reputation for being very lenient and understanding with past-due loans. In fact, they only repossessed two cars and four trucks over the past two years despite hundreds of delinquent accounts. As far as local banks were concerned, First National Bank was considered a "pushover" within the community.

Zack knew that that practice had to end, so he informed his loan officers that they were to send out urgent past-due notices and begin repossessing all vehicles that were more than sixty days past due next month. Zack knew he would lose customers once word got out that First National Bank was cracking down on past-due loans, so he simultaneously cut rates on new vehicle loans in half. Zack also started a massive radio and newspaper advertising campaign for First National Bank's new loan rates. Again, his strategy paid off.

Ninety days after kicking off his campaign, dozens of vehicles were repossessed and resold at auctions, and the loan department had received so many applications that they began to turn away customers with credit scores previously accepted by First National Bank. The community was also buzzing. Car dealers and consumers were praising First National Bank for helping make cars more affordable. On the other hand, competitive banks were complaining that First National Bank was offering artificially low-interest rates to hurt competitors.

Six months after kicking off the campaign, two smaller banks closed, and two more said they would have to sell or close their doors soon. Zack was on cloud nine. He heard some of the whispers within the community that he was "tough" and "ruthless," and he loved it. Zack wanted to be even more ruthless, so he purchased the two banks that were struggling due to his cut-rate loans and put a notice out that he was willing to buy more banks.

After his first year as president of First National Bank, Zack's bank owned 30 percent of the remaining banks in the community after buying five and watching two shut down. As a result of the new banks he purchased, First National Bank inherited a sizable home loan or mortgage business. They had never been in the home-loan business, so this was new and exciting for Zack.

The region was in a multiyear housing boom, and many of the banks were making a lot of money with home loans. Zack was feeling invincible after his vehicle-loan strategy worked so well, and he decided to do something similar with home loans. Zack cut rates and advertised that First National Bank required the lowest down payment for home loans.

For months, new customers came to First National Bank in droves to purchase and refinance their homes. Suddenly, the housing boom came to a screeching halt after mortgage rates rose dramatically in a matter of months. All the other banks raised their loan rates, and Zack followed suit by raising his rates higher than anybody else. Zack knew he had to lock in his profits while interest rates were going up.

Nine months after getting into the home-loan business, Zack noticed more and more customers were getting behind on their loans. Many of the homes were worth less than the loan amount First National Bank provided the homeowners. Zack felt home values would continue to fall, so he began pursuing bank repossession of the homes aggressively to minimize his losses.

Immediately, cries of predatory lending came from the community. The darling of car loans one year prior was now considered one of the most unethical people in the community. Zack was no longer considered "tough" and "ruthless" but was instead considered "a heartless and unethical jerk."

During the past year, Zack purchased his own luxury home, a boat, and two sports cars. Despite some negative comments, Zack was pretty successful, and he wanted everyone to know it. He was not going to let some ruffled feathers bother him. Plus, the ten-year reunion was at the end of the month, and Zack was sure he was finally one of the most successful graduates from his Liberty High School class.

One morning in his office at work, he received a phone call that changed his fortunes.

Zack's assistant, Jackie, buzzed him and said, "I have someone on the line who says he needs to speak with you, and it's urgent."

"You know I'm busy, Jackie. Who is it?"

"The gentleman said he is with the Federal Trade Commission's Predatory Lending Division. Are we in trouble?"

"No, we are not in trouble, Jackie! Tell him I'm just getting back to my office and pass him to me in a minute," Zack yelled.

Zack knew why this man was calling, and his heart sank. He was going to have to answer some difficult questions. So he stood up, straightened his suit, cleared his throat, and took the call. It was Zack's worst fear. Two members of the FTC were coming to visit him next month to investigate complaints of predatory lending they had received from several members of the community.

Zack felt sick, so he left the office early that day. Once he got home, he logged on to his social-media sites, and then his day got even worse. The Liberty High School social-media reunion page was blowing up with hundreds of comments. Joe was sending his regrets that he could not attend the reunion because his Major League Baseball team was going to the playoffs. Joe also said he missed everyone and hoped they would all root for his team in the playoffs. The number of comments in the post telling Joe how much they *missed him, loved him, wished him luck, were new fans,* etc. was making Zack feel even more nauseous. He was so close to topping Joe, and now Zack was getting investigated for a crime while Joe was going to be on national TV as a sports hero.

Zack banged his head on the keyboard for nearly a minute. Then, he went to bed for the night at seven thirty just wanting the day to end.

The Change

On the day of the ten-year, high-school reunion that Zack had been looking forward to for the last decade was finally here, but Zack was not happy to be there. He moped around for the first hour as he sat at a table with more people he despised in high school. Finally, he got up to look for any familiar faces in the room. On his way to get more punch, he saw his old neighbor, Todd. Zack perked up for the first time as he walked over to talk to Todd.

"Hey, Todd. I've meant to call you. It's great to see you."

"Zack, great to see you, too. It is great to see everyone again."

"Yeah, I guess," Zack lied. "I heard you're a pastor now down at the Light of the Valley church."

"I'm the youth pastor, and I love it. Never going to be rich, but I love what I do and wouldn't change it for anything.

"Talk about success. How about you? I think you may have achieved your goal, Mr. Bank President. You've built yourself a nice success story in a short period of time," Todd said with a genuine smile, obviously not knowing what happened in the past few months.

Zack was still feeling the sting of the pending investigation. He wanted to yell at Todd for not knowing, but he knew Todd was the most honest and caring person he knew, so he didn't do it. Instead, Zack broke down to Todd.

"Todd, I have to tell you things are not as good as they may appear. I got a little too ambitious, and now I think I'm headed for trouble. Like my dad always said, 'I will reap what I sow.'"

Zack dumped the past three years of his life on Todd, and as usual, Todd listened patiently and counseled Zack.

After a long conversation, Todd noticed that many of his friends were leaving the reunion, so he told Zack he had to catch up with a few people before they left. As he was beginning to walk away, he asked Zack, "Will I see you at Light of the Valley next weekend?"

Zack had not attended church since he was in high school, so he was a little shocked at the question. He thought about it and responded, "You know all the stuff going on in my life right now. I don't think now is a good time for me."

Todd flashed his genuine smile again and said, "I couldn't think of a better time for you to go. I'll be looking for you next weekend. Take care, Zack."

"OK," was all Zack could muster as Todd walked to another table of former classmates.

Zack thought about it further and knew Todd was right. Maybe going back to church would help get his mind right and his life back on track. Zack went to Light of the Valley church the next weekend. He had returned for six straight weeks before the investigators came. Zack felt the messages of hope, redemption, and forgiveness were helping give him a greater perspective on his situation. Now he was prepared to be honest and accept accountability with the investigators.

His new attitude and cooperation must have helped because the FTC only issued a fine and some corrective actions for First National Bank. Zack was facing total financial ruin and potentially even some criminal charges, so he was relieved to receive only a fine. Zack was still driven to make lots of money but learned he needed to be much more careful and smart about it in the future.

Several months later, Zack was in church when the lead pastor announced they would be having a special guest the next weekend from a world championship baseball team. The pastor was giddy, and the crowd buzzed, but Zack moaned because that only meant one thing. Joe was coming back to town as the local hero after his team just won the World Series.

Zack found Todd after the service and asked him, "Is Joe coming here next week?"

Todd smiled and said, "Yes, isn't that great? It's not every day someone on a World Series winning team comes to Light of the Valley."

"I don't think I can make it next week, Todd. You know how I feel about Joe, and I still have a lot of stuff to work out. Maybe, the week after."

"Zack, I understand. My advice is to pray about it. Maybe it's time to forgive Joe so you can move on."

"Todd, he bullied me more than anyone else in high school. I don't think I can ever forgive him for that!"

"Zack, I know you have only been coming here for a few months, but you have heard about how forgiveness is for you, not for the person who hurts you. It doesn't mean what was done to you was OK; it just means you are canceling the debt so you can move on."

"I don't think I could ever cancel any type of debt in my line of work," Zack said with a half smile.

"Great point, Mr. Bank President. Seriously, just pray about it, and see where God leads you. Canceling debt is never easy for anyone, but you may need to do it more than most. Zack, just pray about it."

"OK, OK—I get it. I will pray about it," Zack stated as he turned and walked into the parking lot.

"I hope to see you next week, Zack," Todd said with his trademark smile.

Even though Zack had been going back to church, he could not recall ever praying at home. He trusted Todd, so he gave it a shot. He prayed all week and started to have feelings that he had never had before. He was not as bitter about Joe for the first time in his life.

Next Sunday arrived, and Zack decided he could not miss the opportunity to see Joe again, so he went to church. He did not want Joe to see him, so he sat in the upper balcony in the back of the church.

Joe was warmly welcomed when he arrived on stage. After a two-minute standing ovation, the pastor told people to take their seats so he could interview Joe.

After a thrilling video collage of Joe playing in the World Series on the big screens in front of the church, the pastor interviewed Joe on stage. The pastor said to Joe, "Tell us about your journey that got you to where you are today."

Zack thought, *Oh great. Now I have to listen to fifteen minutes about why Joe is great, from Joe.* However, Joe's response shocked Zack.

"It all started when I accepted the Lord Jesus Christ as my Savior," Joe replied.

Zack was shocked to hear that response and was interested to hear more, so he leaned forward over the railing in the front row of the balcony to ensure that he heard Joe correctly.

Joe continued, "I was not a very good person in high school and even my first year in college, but I met a teammate who introduced me to Jesus. Everything changed after that."

Joe and the pastor continued to discuss Joe's transformation and how it had grounded him both personally and professionally. Despite his success on the baseball diamond, Joe said his success with his faith and family was even more important to him. The pastor probed further about the change. Joe responded that he had to do a lot of forgiving and apologizing to get where he was today. Then Joe said something that Zack thought he would never hear.

"I was hurt, so I hurt a lot of people. Even some people in this room. I noticed a guy in the balcony whom I was a real jerk to in high school. I would like to apologize personally to him today."

Joe turned and looked directly at Zack and said, "Zack, would you be willing to come down to the stage today so I can apologize to you?"

Zack felt every set of eyes in the entire church look his way. This was all happening so fast, and Zack was not sure how he felt about Joe apologizing to him in public. After a few seconds of silence that felt like two minutes, Zack stood up and said, "Joe, I appreciate the offer, but it's not necessary for you to apologize to me."

Joe let out a little laugh and said, "I should not have put you on the spot like that. I totally understand, but it would really mean a lot to me if you would come down to the stage."

Zack desired for this unwanted attention on him to end, and he knew if he resisted it would only get worse.

Therefore, Zack walked down the stairs and up to the stage to applause. Once he reached the stage, Joe looked him in the eye and began his apology.

"Zack, I was a total jerk to you in high school. I was getting so much praise and recognition for my athletics from everyone in the community, but not at home. Never at home. At home, I was just a dumb jock that would never amount to anything. So I had a very low self-esteem despite my success on the field. I saw that you were so smart, you were very confident, and I would always see your parents supporting you at games. That made me jealous of you. I picked on you because it made me feel better about my crappy situation at home. I was so wrong to do that. You didn't deserve it, and I can't apologize to you enough for the hurt I have caused you. I am sorry."

Zack was stunned. He felt years of anger toward Joe leaving his body like a deflating balloon. For the first time in his life, Zack felt sincere empathy for Joe. He took the microphone and responded, "Joe, I appreciate the apology. I forgive you. Your debt to me is forgiven!"

Joe was standing next to Zack, so he gave Zack a side-hug on stage.

Zack felt an uncontrollable urge to make things right, so he continued, "However, I also need to repent today. I have been so driven to prove Joe and many others from high school wrong that I have stepped on a lot of people so I could climb higher. I thought becoming wealthy would prove that I was better than everyone. Instead, it blinded me to where real riches comes from—family, friends, and faith. Now I know—and this is going to really hurt—but now I know that I need to return my unjust money to the rightful owners. Starting immediately, I am giving back to the community all the money I made with judgment clouded by greed. You can call me directly if I have wronged you or owe you anything."

The audience clapped and cheered as Zack walked off the stage. He continued to walk right out of the church and stopped. He turned around to look at the church, took a deep breath, and said, "Thank you!"

A few seconds later, Todd walked out and hugged Zack. "Zack, I am so proud of what you did. I know how hard that had to be for you."

"Surprisingly, I feel pretty good about the whole thing. It's like this enormous weight was lifted off my shoulders. Worrying about Joe or making money at any cost was a heavy burden to carry."

"I bet it was. God said His burden is light, and I think you are feeling that for the first time," Todd said, still smiling.

"I think you may be right. Todd, I meant what I said about giving back, and I want to start with you. Light of the Valley does such a great job in the community, and you are such a great youth pastor that I want to donate fifty-thousand dollars to your youth program."

"That's a very generous donation, Zack," Todd said, smiling even more now.

"I couldn't think of a better use for that money, Todd. Thanks again for all your support, guidance, and wisdom over the years."

"You're welcome, Zack."

"I need to get going. I have a lot of work to do to repair the damage I've caused for so many in this community."

Zack was true to his word. Over the next two years, he provided so much for local <u>charities</u> that he received several awards for his generous giving within the community. He also changed his policies at First National Bank. He corrected the financial losses many customers incurred as a result of his actions, personally.

Zack gave so much back that he had to sell his house, boat, and both cars. He bought a used car and moved into a small condo. Money was tight for Zack for the first time in his adult life, but he continued to do what was right after he forgave and was forgiven. He even volunteered as a teacher's aide in Todd's youth ministry on weekends.

Zack was never happier in his life.

Overview

This story is a modern retelling of the parable of Zacchaeus the tax collector in Luke 19:1–10.

In this version, Zack is Zacchaeus, the tax collector, and Joe is Jesus coming into Jericho. Like the parable in the Bible, Zack is wealthy, proud, and short. He climbs a tree to see Jesus. Jesus calls him down from the tree when He sees him. Zacchaeus repents and gives half of his possessions to the poor. Joe also calls Zack down to the stage, where he repents and starts the process of giving his possessions to others in need.

This story shows how Zack realized that his love of stockpiling money to validate himself was wrong and still left him feeling empty. He finally repented his actions.

Moral of the Story: Money is often misunderstood. Money itself is not good or bad—it is neutral. The importance we place on money (it can become an idol for some as it did for Zack) and how it affects our actions is where money can turn from a good to a bad thing. Happiness will come from loving God and people, not money!

THE HAPPY DISHWASHER

Alex paused and noticed the bead of sweat that glided down his face until it reached the tip of his nose and stopped. He watched it hang in the balance for a few seconds, and then like a dog getting out of a bathtub; he shook his head, so the sweat flew off in all directions.

The son of a successful restaurateur, Alex had thought his days of doing dishes were behind him. He was not happy that the new employees did not show up, and all those on the regular weekend crew were at a wedding. It had been months since he had to be in the basement washing dishes.

"Alex, get the lead out so we can get those plates upstairs," his older sister, Sophia, yelled out, dropping even more plates and silverware into the wash basin.

"We have a six-top and then an eight-top waiting to be seated, so you've gotta be a lot faster!" Sophia was the regular dining room manager, and she was not going to let a scheduling glitch get in the way of the stellar service she always provided.

"What about little Nick? Can't he help out a little?" Little Nick, Alex's *older* brother, was the first of three children of Rosa and Nick Sr., who everyone had called "Papa" since the day Nick Jr. was born.

"Excuse me?" snapped Sophia, in the voice that let Alex know he should not have asked. "Nick is upstairs right now, running the kitchen practically by himself. Maybe you should wash dishes a little faster so you can go help him!"

"Yeah, yeah. Whatever! Go back upstairs. You're the one slowing me down!" Alex mumbled loudly, slamming dishes into the dishwasher.

Later that night, the last guest left a little after eleven. The dining room and kitchen were cleaned, and the last of the dishes dried and set up for Monday. Nick went around the restaurant and told his family he wanted to meet with them in the bar.

Nick was standing. Papa and Sophia sat across from him at the high-top table. Alex walked in and helped himself to his favorite mixed drink behind the bar.

While Alex was topping off his drink with lime, Nick said, "I want to thank all of you for coming in on your day off to help out. I know it's not easy to give up a

Saturday night, especially to come into this madhouse, but that is what we do as a family."

"Where were the—" Alex started, but Nick put up his hand to stop him.

Clearly aggravated, Nick continued, "Like I said, I am sorry you had to give up your Saturday night, but I will fix this, so it does not happen again." Nick took a couple of steps toward Alex, getting within a few feet of his face, and said, "Was it so hard to come in and help out Sophia and me after all we do for this place? Did you ever think that Dad would rather be home with Mom this weekend after managing restaurants for thirty-six years? I never heard him complain once." Nick was getting louder. His face was turning the shade of red that always signaled that he was not in the mood to play around.

But Alex, too, was tired and angry, and he spilled his drink on the bar as he slammed it down and yelled back, "You chose to stay in this business. But I didn't. You and Sophia are managers, and when I come in, I get stuck unloading trucks, cleaning grease traps, and washing dishes in the basement. I went to college, so I wouldn't have to work in a restaurant all my life! I'm going to become a software developer or whatever I have to do so I don't have to do this anymore."

Sophia chirped quickly, "Then maybe you should have gone to class more often so you could have actually graduated."

"OK," Papa said, motioning down with his hands to stop an argument he had heard too often.

"I couldn't afford to pay for any more classes, so I had to work, and that—"

Nick cut Alex off again. "Sophia and I managed to do both, so—"

"Well, you—" Alex started, leaning in within a few inches of Nick's face.

"I said enough!" Their father jumped in with lightning speed. Everyone was silenced, and Papa continued. "I didn't come in here tonight to help out and then listen to this. We have all been given much by the Lord, and each and every one of you is blessed. Your mom and I worked too hard to give this family everything we have today to sit here and watch my kids attack each other. All of you go home now. Alex, I want to have a word with you before you go."

Nick and Sophia, respecting their father and loving him dearly for all he had given them, did not like to disappoint or upset their dad. So they stood up, gave him a hug, and headed for the front door. Nick said, "I'm locking the door behind me. Dad, can you remember to lock up before you leave?"

"Yes, I will. Have a good night," Papa said in his soothing voice.

Alex was still standing behind the bar near the spilled drink. Papa turned to him and said, "Clean that up, and come over here. I want to talk to you."

Alex did as he was told, leaving the bar to sit across the table from his father. Papa looked Alex in the eyes and said, "I know you don't want to be here, but this is still a family business, so sometimes, we need you to come in and help out. Until you have a full-time job, your mom and I expect you to help your brother and sister. They have worked very hard to keep this place running as smoothly as it does. Do you understand?"

Alex looked down at the table and nodded his head that he understood.

"Do you know why we sold the entire chain of Papa's Family Grill restaurants while you were only twelve years old?" Papa asked Alex.

"Yes, so you could spend more time with your family and provide us with a better life than you and Mom had," Alex replied quickly. He had heard that story a million times, it seemed.

"Exactly," said Papa. "And do you know why we opened up this place even though we didn't have to work anymore?"

Alex paused and said, "No, why exactly did you start a new restaurant after you sold Papa's Grill? You didn't need to work like this anymore."

Papa leaned back in his chair, crossed his arms, and smiled when he said, "Because this is what we do. We wanted to teach all of you how to build and run a successful restaurant. I wanted to do it as a family."

"But, Dad, you know that is not something I ever wanted to do. No offense, but this just isn't for me. I want to build my own successful business, just like you and Mom did, but I don't want to be in the restaurant industry. I have some ideas of my own, and I need time to work them out. Don't you get it?" Alex asked, exasperated.

"Yes, I get it," Papa said calmly. "Your mom and I just want to help you in any way we can, so how can we help you?"

This was the moment Alex had been thinking about for a long time but never worked up the courage to ask his father. He knew the timing now was perfect, so Alex straightened up in his chair and cleared his throat. His voice was quiet and steady. "You know how you always said you had put away some of the money from the sale of Papa's Grill for all three of us—to help us start our own businesses?"

"Yes, I do," Papa said, knowing where the conversation was going.

"Well, I would like my portion of the money now so I can finish school and start my own mobile app development company." Alex stared directly into his father's eyes, waiting for an answer.

Papa paused and said, "Alex, you have always been the creative dreamer of the family. We have always supported your dream to do something different. You're twenty-six now, so it is time for you to start building a career of your own. Are you sure this mobile-programming thing is the business you want to start? It seems a little risky."

Alex jumped out of his seat and said, "Yes! I am one hundred percent sure. That is what I have always wanted to do. I was getting pretty good at it just before I had to drop out when I ran out of tuition money. So what do you think?"

"It is a lot of money just to hand over, so I have to talk to your mom about it and will let you know. It's after midnight now, so let's go home to get some sleep."

"I'll head home in a bit. I'm meeting Christo and George."

Papa said, "You're going out with those guys? Will you be at church tomorrow?"

"Oh, um, of course. I'll see you there."

Papa smiled and opened the door to let Alex out. "Good night, son. I'll see you in the morning." Papa checked to ensure all the other doors were locked as he had so many other times in his life. He could not stop thinking about Alex's question, and it was looming heavy on his heart. So before he locked the final door and went home, Papa sat down at the bar, put his head down, and prayed.

The next day, Alex's mom, Rosa, was setting the table for their traditional Sunday family dinner. She saw Alex come in the back door and said, "Hello, honey. I hope you're hungry."

"I'm starving."

"Good, I made your favorite. I didn't see you at church today. Did you go to another service?" Rosa asked, already knowing the answer.

"No, I didn't make it. Something came up, but it's all good now. So did you and Dad talk?" Alex asked, changing the subject.

"Yes, we did. He will let you know later what we decided. Dinner is in twenty minutes," Rosa snapped, wanting to change the subject herself.

After dinner, Alex's parents played with their grandkids. Nick's baby girl was eighteen months, and Sophia had a two-year-old son. Both stole the hearts of their grandparents. After the grandkids had fallen asleep on the couch, their parents placed them carefully in the car to go home.

After they had left, Alex asked his dad if he had the time to talk about the money. Papa agreed, and they met in the living room.

"Did you and Mom talk?" Alex asked nervously.

"Yes, we did," his father replied. "This is not easy because Little Nick is thirty-two and has a young family, and Sophia is twenty-nine and also has a family. They both have done everything we have ever asked of them, and they are working so hard to maintain the restaurant business. Neither has ever asked for money."

Alex was concerned with the direction of the conversation, so he interjected, "But, I am—"

"Let me finish," Papa said, putting his hand up. He was slow and steady in speech as he continued. "Even though your older brother and sister have never asked for any money, they know they will be rewarded for staying in the family business. You, on the other hand, wish to do something different, something you are passionate about. Your mom and I have always said we would support you, and we want to keep our word. Therefore, we will transfer the money we set aside into your account so you can go back to school and start your business."

"Really? Wow! That's awesome!" Alex gave his father a hug and then jumped up to hug his mom, who had just walked into the room. "Thank you so much for believing in me. I have so much to do, so I need to get home now and figure out when I can sign up for classes. Bye, Mom and Dad. I love you!"

"Haven't heard that in a while," said Papa, as Alex ran out the door.

"I know," said Rosa, "but it is sure nice to hear it and see him that happy. I just hope he can get on the right path and stay away from those guys who drink every night of the week, especially now that Alex has money in his pocket."

The Slide

A month had passed since Alex received the money, and he was showing up less and less for family dinners on

Sunday. One day, Alex showed up at his parents' house with his beloved dog, Hercules. Hercules was a red Doberman that Alex bought as a puppy two years earlier and was Alex's best friend. After Alex and Hercules had come in the back door, he yelled out for his mom and dad to come into the kitchen.

When they both arrived, Alex asked, "Could you watch Hercules for a week or two while I go on a quick vacation before I head back to school full time? I need to blow off some steam before I start hitting the books hard."

His mom answered first. "Yes, of course. We love Hercules. Who are you going with, and where are you going?"

Alex knew they would not like his answer, but he replied, "I'm going with George and Christo. We're not sure where we're going yet. We want to do something spontaneous since we may not get a chance to do this again."

"I don't think a spontaneous vacation with those guys is a good idea, Alex," his father responded quickly.

"I know, I know," Alex said as he paced back and forth in the kitchen. "I know I've done a lot of stupid things with those guys in the past, but we're all growing up and want to get together and celebrate one last time. I'll be back in two weeks max to get Hercules and begin my classes."

"Better get it out of your system because you have some growing up to do. We will see you in two weeks,"

Papa said, concerned already about what Alex had planned.

One week later, Sophia was planning to tell the family that she was expecting her second child at Sunday dinner. She tried to contact Alex to confirm that he was coming to dinner, but he did not respond. At dinner, Sophia noticed Hercules and asked, "Where's Alex?" Papa told the rest of the family that he gave Alex his "new business" money so he could go back to school and Alex was taking a quick vacation. Sophia and Nick's heads both snapped up with jaws open wide. After seeing the indifferent look on Papa's face, Nick just shook his head and said, "Unbelievable." He began eating again while Sophia could only muster a "Wow! I wasn't expecting that," before she turned her attention back to feeding her daughter.

A couple of weeks later, Nick ran into another bind at the restaurant. He thought Alex would be back home by now, so Nick left him several texts and voicemail messages asking him to come in but got no response. Only thirty minutes into the shift, Nick was livid and had no choice but to call his father.

"I hate to have to ask you this, Papa, but could you come down to the restaurant as soon as you can to give us a hand? Your son blew us off again, so I am out of options right now." Nick was so angry that his voice cracked. "What's going on with Alex? Did he just take the money and run?"

"Sure, I'll be there in a few minutes. I don't know what's wrong with Alex." Papa was hurt about the way Alex was treating his family. Before leaving for the restaurant, Papa left Alex a message asking for a return call but did not hear back from him.

Another week had passed when Papa noticed one morning that he had received a voicemail message in the middle of the night. It was from Alex, who sounded severely intoxicated. Papa could barely make out what he was saying, except that Alex was with George and Christo and that they were going to spend some more time traveling to "unwind and find some creative inspiration" for the next mobile game.

Alex mumbled on the message, "Tell Sophia congratulations for her new kid. Tell Hercules I miss him. Tell Little Nick I don't do restaurants anymore unless I'm ordering takeout." Papa could not make out the rest. However, he could hear a lot of partying in the background before Alex finally found the End Call button.

Papa was angry and hurt. He suspected something like this might happen because Alex had struggled with excessive drinking in the past. Alex always liked to be the life of the party. Papa had known giving the money to Alex could send him into a few different directions, so he prayed he would make the right decisions, but that did not appear to be the case.

At dinner the following Sunday, Papa told the family that Alex had called. He left out the part about Alex being so drunk he could barely speak, but he did tell them he was traveling to search for new ideas for mobile apps. Sophia and Nick saw right through that. "We're sorry he's doing this to the both of you," Sophia offered. "You worked so hard to give him money that he could have used to build a life for himself, and he's just drinking it away, and who knows what else."

"I'm sorry, too," Papa said sullenly. "Let's just pray for him and hope he sees the error of his ways, so he comes to his senses." No one spoke another word during dinner.

Several months had passed since Alex left that voicemail message for his father. He had settled down twelve-hundred miles from home. Alex was drinking and using drugs every day, spending lavishly, and buying alcohol for everyone at clubs and parties. He was the life of the party, for sure, but his lifestyle burned up all the money his parents had given him. The eternal party was quickly over.

Alone and bored one night, Alex called a girl he met at a club. She had sold him drugs before. He was out of money and thought the girl was kind of cute, so he tried to charm her into coming over and bringing "some party favors." She was interested not in Alex but only in "getting paid cash money for those party favors." Desperate, Alex negotiated that he would pay her double because his "family had money" and he could get it soon, so she agreed to come over.

Alex ran excitedly to let the girl in when she knocked on the door, but she was not alone. Several large men burst into Alex's apartment the instant he opened the door. It happened so fast that Alex was not exactly sure what was going on. He felt the kicks and punches and ended up face down on his couch. Alex noticed potato chip crumbs and the smell of stale beer in the cushions, as one of the men drove a forearm into Alex's neck. When Alex felt cool metal on the back of his head, he knew he was in real trouble.

"Where's it at, rich boy?" the man demanded.

Alex knew what they wanted, so he yelled into the couch cushions, "I don't have any money here. I said that just to get her to come over."

"Bad move, bro. That's going to cost you."

Alex tightened every muscle in his body in anticipation of more punches or, worse yet, the sound of a trigger as it's pulled. Instead, nobody said a word, but Alex could hear a lot of movement in his apartment.

Finally, they put a pillowcase over Alex's head and beat him again before taking him to their car. They drove for just a few minutes and then dropped Alex off in an alley. Alex was told, "Look, bro, you are lucky we don't waste you right now. If you tell anyone or come back to your apartment, we'll kill you. Ya got that?"

Alex believed they would kill him, so he never went back and took up residence on the streets. Soon, he was constantly shaking due to withdrawals from daily use of drugs and alcohol.

Eventually, the substances were detoxed from his system, helping Alex think more clearly about what he had done to his parents. Alex really wanted to talk to his father but felt too ashamed. He spent his days huddled near doorways of local businesses, asking strangers for food and money.

Nights were getting cooler, so Alex walked a couple of miles to a community food bank and kitchen. He arrived during mealtime and ate some soup, which he previously despised because "it was not real food." A volunteer asked to sit next to him and said enthusiastically, "Hi. I'm Roger. What's your name?"

"Alex."

"Hi, Alex. This facility doesn't provide a place to sleep but does offer other helpful resources. Do you need any warm clothes or blankets? Can I help you with anything?" Roger asked.

The question seemed to linger like a hot-air balloon on a calm summer day. Then it hit Alex. *I am homeless and in a soup kitchen, looking for warm blankets.* He had it good back home and really hurt the people who loved him the most.

Alex looked over at Roger. "Do you know how much I would love to wash dishes right now?"

Roger was confused by the question but glanced at the kitchen area and said, "I'm sure the folks here would find something here for you to wash if you really want to."

Alex replied, "No, not here. At my family's restaurant."

Roger smiled and said, "Oh, you have a family? Are you able to contact them?"

Alex looked down and spoke to the table. "No, I could never ask them for help again. I've screwed up too bad this time, and I am too ashamed to face them right now. Anyway, I—" Alex stopped himself and then said, "You know what? I would love to have some extra blankets."

Roger smiled and got up from the table. He came back a few minutes later with two blankets, a box of granola bars, and a large bottle of water. "Here," Roger said. "Take all of this. It will help you during this cold spell."

Roger walked away but then turned back to Alex and said, "I hope to see you here again sometime. I volunteer twice a month." Roger put his hands in his pockets and looked Alex right in the eye. "And, Alex, don't underestimate your father. I'm sure he loves you more than you know, so think about giving him a call sometime."

Alex was happy to have the extra blankets, but he struggled emotionally with what Roger said about calling Papa. Deep down, Alex knew his father still loved him, but he also knew he had really hurt his family. A cold sidewalk and steady diet of cinnamon-raisin granola bars were much more appealing than facing his family right now. Alex left the food bank and walked back to his usual spot under the exhaust fan near a hotel's loading dock. He positioned his makeshift mattress in a corner and slowly drifted to sleep.

Alex continued to endure the challenges of trying to survive on the streets. One of his blankets was stolen, and he got into a fight that resulted in a black eye and swollen lip. Alex realized it had been two weeks since he last went to the soup kitchen and thought Roger might be there, so he walked there that evening. Again, he got there in time for a meal. He looked around as he stood in the cafeteria-style line. He ate the pork and beans and then picked up a coat and another blanket. Alex was disappointed that he did not see Roger.

Instead of trekking the miles back to his usual sleep spot, Alex walked around the corner from the center and went behind an old church. He lied down on a concrete bench and chuckled when he looked upward and noticed the cross at the top of the church. He said to himself out loud, "God, I know my dad always prays to you. But even after all those years my parents forced me to go to church, I still have my doubts. Anyway, I could really use you now." Alex was talking louder and faster. "I know you probably don't help people like me, but I really hurt my family and don't know what to do. Since you know it all, please tell me what I should do."

Alex fixed his eyes on the cross a while longer, waiting for God to speak to him directly in that deep Darth Vader voice he always figured God had. After several minutes of silence, Alex said, "That's what I thought." He stared up at the partly cloudy sky until he fell into a slumber and snoozed peacefully through the night. It was the first time since finding himself homeless that he had slept more than two hours at a time.

The next morning, he milled around the area and killed time during the day in a park nearby. Alex was the first person in line when the kitchen opened that evening. As soon as he walked through the door, he saw Roger. A grin stretched across Alex's face as Roger walked over to him. "Hey, Alex. Good to see you again. How are you doing?"

"I've been better," Alex said, still smiling. "Do you know that the employees who wash dishes in the basement of my family's restaurant have it better than me?"

Roger just stared at Alex, without uttering a word.

Alex continued, "I used to think that was below me, but I can't take this anymore. If my family will take me back, I'll wash dishes in that hot basement for the rest of my life." Alex stopped, expecting a response from Roger. "Aren't you going to say anything?"

Roger smiled and offered his cell phone to Alex. "Wanna call him now?"

The Return

Alex took Roger's phone and walked outside to the church's concrete bench, where he had slept the night before. It was quiet there, and Alex wanted complete privacy for what he was about to do. He dialed Papa's number and then paused. He took a deep breath and hit Send.

It seemed like an eternity, but on the third ring, his dad answered. "Hello?"

Alex froze. Warm emotions streamed through him at the sound of his father's voice. He was choked up and did not know what to say.

Again, he heard his dad. "Hello. Is anyone there?"

Afraid Papa would hang up, Alex managed to summon enough air from his lungs to say, "Dad, it's me. It's Alex." Alex braced himself because he was certain his father would yell or sigh in utter disappointment.

But Papa's reaction was quite the opposite. He was ecstatic to have a call from his wayward son. "Alex! I am so happy to hear from you." Alex could hear the emotion in his father's voice. "Are you OK?"

Alex was not sure why, but his father's concerned words had him suddenly sobbing uncontrollably. A massive wave of guilt came crashing over him, and he needed to purge every last bit of shame. "No, Dad," Alex managed. "I am not OK. I really screwed up this time, worse than ever. I lost all the money you gave me—drinking, drugs, gambling—you name it, I probably did it. I have been robbed and beaten up more times than I can count, and I've been sleeping on concrete while begging for money. I am so sorry for what I did to all of you, and I just can't take this anymore. Can I come back and wash dishes at the restaurant? I promise I will never complain or do this again."

Alex was nearly out of breath, waiting for his father's response. He heard nothing and wondered if his father had hung up on him. "Hello? Papa, are you there?"

"Yes, I am here," Papa said, in his typical soothing voice. "Alex, you need to come home now. Where are you?" Alex revealed his location, and his dad said he would arrange for a bus ticket the next morning.

"Dad, I can't thank you enough. I am so, so sorry. I promise this will never happen again. Seriously, thank you."

Papa replied calmly, "You're welcome, son. I will see you in a couple of days."

Alex was a little shocked by his father's response, but he was ecstatic to be going home. He returned Roger's phone, thanked him, and told him about the conversation with his father. As always, Roger was supportive and told him, "Your father will always love you, no matter what you have done. Go home, and change your ways to show your father how much you love him." Roger then vanished back into the kitchen.

Alex went back to the cold concrete bench near the church and lied down. He could feel himself falling asleep quickly, but he sat up suddenly and looked at the cross atop the church. Smiling, he said, "Thank you!" Alex slept soundly through the night.

The next morning, Alex picked up his ticket, boarded the bus, and began the two-day journey back home. He was nervous about how everyone would react to him upon his return, but the thought of sleeping in a warm bed and taking a hot shower was too appealing to turn back now.

The bus arrived thirty minutes early, and Alex looked in the parking lot to see if anyone was there to pick him up. He did not see anyone, so he walked to his parents' home fifteen blocks away. After a twenty-minute walk, he arrived at his parents' house, found the spare key hidden in the same spot since Nick Jr. was a teenager, and let himself in. Immediately, he was greeted by Hercules, who was jumping on him, whining and running around the house in excitement. Alex hugged Hercules and started crying again. "I am so sorry for leaving you like that. Never again!"

Alex took a shower, and he felt clean for the first time in months. He found some clean clothes in the guest room, which was his old bedroom.

He was not sure where everyone was, but he wanted to see his family, so he started walking to the restaurant.

Papa and Rosa had gone to the bus station to pick up Alex but did not know the bus had arrived early. Once they realized Alex was not there, Papa assumed he was walking home. So they drove around the streets where they were most likely to find Alex. As soon as Papa spotted Alex, he was so excited that he pulled the car off the road, jumped the curb, and stopped on the sidewalk. Papa hopped out of the car, ran up to Alex, and hugged him. Alex's mom joined in on the hugging.

By this time, all three were crying, and Alex was even more confused by his parents' reaction. He had betrayed his whole family, squandering their hard-earned money on drugs, gambling, and alcohol.

Rosa spoke first. "Alex, we are so happy you are back. We missed you so much!"

Still feeling ashamed, but at the same time moved by his parents' unconditional love for him, Alex replied softly, "I thought everyone would be really mad at me."

Papa said, "The important thing is that you are here now and seem to be OK."

"I am," said Alex.

"Great," said Papa. "Let's go to the restaurant and celebrate."

It was a typical Tuesday night, so the restaurant was not very crowded. Papa was excited and walked through the entrance shouting, "My son is back!

Papa spoke to the hostess and told her to call Nick, Sophia, and some close family friends to come down to the restaurant and celebrate Alex's return.

Sophia received the call from the hostess. When she heard about the celebration, she was confused and angry. She thought Alex was coming back home to be reprimanded and to ask them for forgiveness—not thrown a party the moment he returned. Upset, Sophia called Nick to see what he thought.

Nick was livid. "I can't believe it! That can't be right. I'm going over there right now!" Nick stormed out of his house.

Meanwhile, at the restaurant, everyone was congratulating Alex on his return. Privately, his father said to him, "I know we have a lot to talk about later when the time is right, but I do have one question now: what made you call me a couple of days ago?"

Alex was a little stumped by the question, and after some thought, he replied, "This guy Roger who volunteered at the homeless shelter really got me thinking. I told him I was too ashamed to speak to you again, and he said never to underestimate the love of my father. It hit me right then that although I really screwed up, you still love me."

Papa replied, "I will have to thank this Roger if I ever meet him."

"I think there was another reason, too," Alex confided. "You know how you dragged me to church all those times? Well, I think God might have actually answered my prayers. I had prayed the night before I called, asking Him to tell me what to do. I didn't hear anything that night, but the next day when I saw Roger, I really felt like I needed to call you right then and there. It was weird. I'm not sure, but I think maybe God had some-thing to do with it."

"I am sure He answered your prayers," Papa replied with certainty. "My prayers were answered, too."

At that, Papa hugged Alex and yelled, "More hot wings for my boy. He hasn't eaten well for months!"

Papa paused and said to Alex, "I prefer you don't drink tonight."

"Don't worry, I don't think I will be drinking any-time in the future," Alex replied. "I detoxed the hard way and don't ever want to do that again!"

A few minutes later, Nick stormed into the restau-rant and saw all the commotion in the lounge—people crowding around Alex and patting him on the back. Nick could not believe it. Alex was always getting into trouble, and this time, he even blew all the money his parents had saved while working countless hours in the restaurant business to provide a good life for their chil-dren. Now Alex was penniless and homeless, and it ap-peared his parents couldn't be happier.

On the other hand, Nick had always done what his parents wanted. He had worked in their restaurants since he could walk, never got into any trouble, and was largely the reason why their current restaurant was so successful. His parents never threw a party like that for him, so his anger was building.

Nick decided to confront his parents, approaching his mom first. "What's going on? Why are we having a party for Alex after he blew all your money and came home broke?"

Rosa was a little startled to see Nick's reaction, but she placed her hand gently on his arm and said, "We'll have plenty of time to address Alex's sins, but for now, we want to celebrate because he is well and has returned home. Grab something to eat. Join us."

Nick was in no mood to celebrate the return of the family's troublemaker, and he was sure his father would understand his point of view. "Dad, what is going on here? Why are you throwing a party for Alex after all he has done to me, Sophia, Mom, and especially, you?"

Papa responded, "We are just so happy that your brother has returned safely. We will address what he has done another time."

"I know that!" Nick yelled. "I heard the same thing from Mom, but I still don't get it. I have done everything you've asked me to do my entire life. I try never to disappoint you and Mom—and you have never thrown a party like this for me. Should I take all the money you promised me and put it down my throat like Alex did?"

Papa smiled. "Look, son, you have always been with me, and everything I have is yours. We had to celebrate this happy day for your brother was dead and has come back to life! He was lost, but now he is found."

Nick turned around and walked out of the restaurant while the party continued for Alex.

Several months later, Alex was excited to be working as an assistant manager in the restaurant. He worked the longest and worst hours. He even washed dishes again—happily, when needed. Alex understood that he was part of a family business, and he wanted to be a good member of the family.

Sophia and Little Nick were having trouble forgiving Alex. Alex knew it would be a long process, but he knew that his mother and father forgave him completely. Alex knew he could always depend on a father's love.

Overview

This story is the modern rendition of the parable of the lost son, perhaps more commonly known as the prodigal son, in Luke 15:11–32.

In this modern-day retelling of the story, Papa is the father, Alex is the prodigal son, and Nick is the jealous brother. In both stories, the parable demonstrates that God, our Father in Heaven, loves us and will accept, at any time, all who are willing to repent, regardless of what they have done.

It also shows, similar to the jealous brother in both stories, that keeping score on good deeds is not enough. God wants your heart, mind, and soul—not just skill in following rules. God sent His Son, Jesus, to change sinners, so Heaven rejoices every time a lost sinner returns.

Moral of the Story: It is never too late to turn to God, no matter what you have done. He is ready to throw a party and welcome you back into the family whenever you take that first step back toward Him.

HOPE CONTINUED

It is my hope that everyone who reads *Hope Refreshed* is entertained. It is my prayer that anyone who could use some peace, hope or inspiration in his or her life can find a sliver of it in this collection of stories.

I hope you enjoyed *Hope Refreshed,* and if you do, a review on Amazon is always appreciated.

Hope Refreshed is the first book of the **Modern Parables Collection**. I will be launching additional books with Bible parables retold as modern stories. You can find more information at **www.RobertGoluba.com** regarding new releases, exclusive offers, future projects and general discussion on my books. I hope to see you there!

Prayer of Hope

Heavenly Father, your abundant grace, and love are clear for all to see.

I know your Son died on the cross for all our sins. He died for me.

The fight with temptation and evil is ferocious, like a boxer in a ring.

With you, I know everything is possible; you can do anything.

I know you are always with me when times are good as well as bad, day or night.

And despite life's troubles, since you are with me, I know everything will be all right.

You love everyone, and you can change any heart. Nothing is out of your scope.

I know you love me just the way I am now, and for that reason, I have eternal hope!

ACKNOWLEDGMENTS

I would like to thank my wife for being my soul mate in this spiritual journey through life and for her endless support in letting me find "my purpose." I want to thank my mom for giving me the foundation that Jesus is my savior and both of my parents for supporting me in everything I do. I want to thank my former teacher at Streator High School, Roy Swanberg, for writing one comment on an essay that lit my flame for writing that never went out.

I also want to thank the pastors, staff, and the entire congregation at Sun Valley Community Church in Gilbert, Arizona, for opening my eyes, my mind, and my heart that I have a Savior and brothers and sisters in Christ.

Lastly, I want to thank my savior, Jesus Christ, for blessing me with the most amazing wife, kids, parents, siblings, extended family, and friends anyone could wish for.

ABOUT THE AUTHOR

Robert Goluba was born and raised Central Illinois, where he attended college, served in the Army National Guard, and met his wife. At age thirty, after a self-diagnosed allergy to snow, he moved to sunny Gilbert, Arizona, where he now lives with his beautiful wife and two daughters. He enjoys hiking, hunting for scorpions with a black light, football, night swims, and golf. God is good!